The Royal Diaries

KAZUNOMIYA

PRISONER OF HEAVEN

BY KATHRYN LASKY

Scholastic Inc. New York

Kyoto, Japan
The Imperial Palace
1858

Kisaragi February 25, 1858
Kyoto, Japan
The Imperial Palace
The Time When Buds Begin to Swell

I was born in the year of the Fire Horse, and no matter what they do, that fact cannot be changed. But, oh, how they try! For a girl to be born in the year of the Fire Horse it is a bad omen. So they say. We are considered to be dangerous — too powerful for men. And for me, born a few months after my father's death, that makes it a doubly bad omen. So my half brother the Emperor Komei ordered that my birthday be changed. I am truly twelve, but they made me thirteen — for good fortune, and to tame the Fire Horse inside me. But sometimes the Fire Horse flares as it just did a few minutes ago when I was caught not tending to my brush painting and listening in on my mother. Oh, was Auntie mad!

"You pay attention to the Four Gentlemen. It is the Way of the Gentlemen that you need to learn," Auntie Umi muttered this as she slid the paper *shoji* screen aside to scold me.

Then she disappeared behind it. I can see her shadow now, and that of my mother's on the other side. Their heads bend toward each other. And then they scurry off. Their long hair streams behind them on the floor like twin rivers. I hear the whisk of their kimonos blend with their low voices.

I am not to hear. I am not to know. But there is trouble here in the palace. My half brother the Emperor is angry, very angry. This much I know. And still I am not to know anything. Instead, I am to turn my attention to the Four Gentlemen. They are not real men, of course. They are not even human beings. They are the four brushstrokes of the *sumi-e* ink paintings. There is the bamboo stroke, the stroke of the wild orchid, the stroke of the chrysanthemum, and the stroke of the wild plum. They are said to represent all the forms and the shapes of the universe, and with them one can paint anything.

But I prefer writing on these pages of rice paper and slipping them into my embroidered cases. I have filled one case already and now will begin a new one. It is actually an old one of my mother's that was given to her on the occasion of her girl's clothing ceremony, when she finished with the trousers and clothing of childhood and began to wear a kimono.

As a princess, I am expected to learn this art of ink painting. And even my brother the Emperor is, in truth, expected only to learn such arts as painting and poetry. But he has learned something more now. And he is furious. He stays in his everyday palace, the *Otsune-goten*, and smolders in the Chamber of the Tiger like a volcano about to explode, like a dragon about to spit fire. It is dragons that he thinks about. It is dragons that consume him. For although it was almost five years ago that the black dragon ships came from the West, carrying the devils with white faces, our lives began to change then and now they might never be the same. A treaty has been signed with these white devils who are also called Americans. The shogun, the big general, signed it. And no one told my brother the Emperor. No one ever tells us anything. You see, we are Gods, descended from the divine sun goddess *Amaterasu*. We live here in the Heavenly Palace, Kyoto Gosho. As Gods we cannot know, we cannot act. We are rarely even permitted to leave our palace. We are prisoners of heaven. And this is our hell. "Our hell," I whisper very quietly to the *ningyo*, the dolls who stand on my doll altar.

Later

Auntie laughed. Thank goodness. I did attend to the Four Gentlemen. But when she returned and saw that I had dipped my brush onto the inkstone to make the pictures of a dragon she said, "Aah, you use the bamboo stroke. Now you must practice those strokes beyond the Gentlemen. Time to learn the bird stroke, for how will you make the dragon's spines?"

Auntie's hands are old and gnarled but when she holds the brush they make the quickest, most precise strokes. *One-two-three-four-five.* She pressed wedge-shaped strokes on my dragon's back, and spines instantly grew. "Tell me the story of the dragon ships," I asked as I watched the dragon take shape on the paper.

"Chikako," she says to me. "I tell you this story a million times. Now is not the time." Her brow furrowed.

"Yes, it is. I shall roast you some beans — beans and green tea." Auntie squeezed her eyes shut until they were little wrinkly seams in her old face. Her nostrils pinched as she sniffed the imaginary fragrance of roasting beans. Auntie could not resist. She loves beans. I sent Keiko, my serving maid, to fetch more coals for the brazier and, of course, the beans. Auntie told me the story of the time the ships came. It was five years ago. I hardly remember. I was only seven — really seven, not eight as they like to pretend.

*   *   *

I turned the beans in the pan, parching them carefully. "And you were in Shimoda visiting your brother," I prompted her to begin.

"Yes, I was visiting my brother by the sea. And the ships really did look like dragons with fire and smoke coming from them. But they never burned up. Many thought of that old folktale that says when there is smoke coming from above the water, it is made by clams. Some clams!" Auntie snorted. "No, devils with white faces they were! And all the fishermen pulled in their nets. Rumors spread like wildfire — barbarians come to invade us, our sacred land. All the alarms were sounded. Temple bells clanged, the speediest of messengers were sent to the shogun in Edo."

But then Auntie Umi, who has told me this story a hundred times, began to shake. "Is something bad happening now, Auntie?"

"We don't know. We don't know." Her eyes, like two little raisins in the puffy folds of her skin, were lit with fear. "We know nothing here in the palace. But the Emperor is very angry. The shogun makes all the decisions. He is supposed to serve the Emperor, but I think he serves only himself. Americans come. The big American *daimyo* Harris comes and makes this thing called a treaty."

"What is a treaty?" I asked.

"I don't know. But it is not good."

"Will we die?"

"Of course we will die. We all die someday. Even Gods die." She paused. Then in a smaller voice. "Even Gods die, Kazunomiya."

Chikako is my nickname. Kazunomiya is my real name. It is too long a name for such a short girl. So no one ever calls me that, except sometimes Auntie when she is deadly serious.

When Auntie left I felt terrible. Auntie Umi is my lady-in-waiting. She is not really my aunt. But she is my mother's best friend, and she must watch me because my mother must constantly watch herself. It is hard to explain but although we live in this Palace of Heaven, there are devils — court ladies who envy my mother. It was much easier when we lived in the home of my mother's father. But now we have been called here to live at the palace within the Imperial court. It has been rebuilt after the last fire a few years ago. I say "the last fire" for there have been so many. When palaces and houses are built from paper and wood, when there is rice straw for floors, fire is drawn to them like bees to honey.

My father was the late Emperor Ninko. And my mother was his favorite consort, or *nyogo*. She was even more of a favorite than his first wife, the mother of the present Emperor Komei. We now call this woman Empress Mother or sometimes the Dowager Empress. She lives here as well. And although Komei's wife, Kujo, prefers my mother, she must act as if she does not in order to please Komei's mother, her mother-in-law. Oh, it is all so complicated. We do not, thankfully, have to live in the *nishibashi*, which is where many of the court ladies and the *nyogo* live. I couldn't stand it. All they do is gossip and plot intrigues. Just a year ago, there were rumors of poison. Yes, someone was going to try to poison my mother. But my mother has good friends who help her and protect her. Auntie Umi is one, but she is awfully old and a bit deaf. So she is not such a good spy. But she is good for me. She is my best friend as well. And now I have upset her with my talk of dragon ships and dying. No more. I shall be the Perfect Princess. I shall make a list of promises of good behavior for the Perfect Princess and write the characters in my best calligraphy. I start now.

1) Attend to the Four Gentlemen daily.
2) Observe most carefully the changes between the winter solstice and the spring equinox and make *waka* poems, one each day if I can.
3) Study the old *waka* masters diligently.

4) Remember to put rice powder on my face every time I leave my apartments to go to the main reception halls.

5) Pay good attention to my music master, Sensei Shoshitsu, and practice at least four times for each lesson. To play a string instrument like the *koto* even half well, demands hours and hours of practice. To master, it takes a lifetime, or so my sensei says.

Yayoi March 1, 1858

Only two days until Girls' Day! Auntie and I must carefully go over the *ningyo* on my doll altar to make sure their clothes are proper and neat for display. I keep them here in my sleeping chamber all year long, but on Girls' Day we bring them into the main salon of the apartments I share with my mother and put them on a higher altar. I have, of course, Emperor and Empress dolls and several court ladies and one who is serving *sake*. The Empress's kimono needs stitching. We call Keiko, my serving girl, to summon the doll seamstress, Fujiko. Fujiko seems no bigger than a doll herself, and she has fingers just slightly fatter than the legs of a cricket.

Later

Fujiko found other rips — ones we couldn't even see. But now my dolls are perfect.

Yayoi March 2, 1858

Auntie came in this morning and asked about my dreams. She always does this. She is a great believer in dreams. I must be a disappointment, for I hardly ever dream. Still she asks.

Yayoi March 3, 1858

We received people in our apartments this morning as Girls' Day has begun. The Emperor came with his wife, Kujo, and Lady Nakayama, who is the mother of his son, little Sachi. Thank heavens, Sachi had the sniffles and was not permitted to attend. He is very wild and last Girls' Day he wanted my samurai doll and was ready to pounce on it until one of his nursemaids stopped him. He's a terrible brat.

My favorite part of Girls' Day is when Auntie and

Mother and I go to the shrine by the Katsura River for the *Nagashi bina* ceremony. *Nagashi* means floating, and we bring our paper dolls — not the dolls from my altar — and float them down the river.

Later

We went to the shrine. It was lovely. This is a very old shrine but few go there. It is Auntie's favorite, even though it is a Shinto shrine and she is a Buddhist. But there are two lovely old weeping willows that bend like elegant ladies into the water with their long sweeps of branches, and there is a rock a few feet from the shore, covered with moss. From it, many tiny plants sprout. Auntie says that a very old spirit lives here, and it is here that we set our paper dolls afloat. They drifted lazily toward the rock. We watched them and drank the flasks of hot tea the servants brought. Finally, we saw the paper dolls spin off into the current. We had rubbed them against our chests so that they would take our worries and regrets with them. My worries and regrets seem so trivial, but I wonder what Auntie's are. They say she was once in love with a man, a samurai whom she was forbidden to marry. And my mother, what are her worries? She was my father the Emperor's favorite *nyogo*, but did she wish to be his first wife rather than his first consort? Did she ever have a forbidden love?

Yayoi March 6, 1858
The Time When the Skylark Sings

SPRING TEA

A cloud of blossoms
A hazy moon
Taste of mist, sweet wind

That is my *waka* for the spring tea that I plan for Auntie and my mother. It is modeled after the greatest of the ancient Japanese poets, Basho. His was better.

Still, I have kept my promises and written many *waka* poems and attended to the Four Gentlemen. I have not practiced so much on the *koto*. But I really have kept most of my promises. This tea is important to me. I am the hostess for my mother, Auntie, and Auntie's niece Tomaki, who has just come to court and caught the Emperor's eye. But this is the most exciting: Tomaki is the cousin of Prince Arisugawa-no-miya Taruhito. And Arisugawa is the man to whom I am betrothed in marriage. Yes, when we are old enough we shall be married. Since I was four years old this has been so. I have only met him three times, but I like him more each time even though he is somewhat older than I. I thought him quite comely-looking, and he likes to make jokes. So I cannot wait to hear news of him.

When I look out my window into the private garden just beside my apartments, there is a tree called the Princess Tree. Its real name is the Royal Paulwonia. It was planted on the day I was born, and when I marry Arisugawa it shall be cut down and its wood shall be used to make a musical instrument for me, a new pair of clogs, and a fine piece of furniture for our home. In another month, however, its blossoms will open.

This tea is a mere tea party and not true tea ceremony. I think Auntie does not quite approve of such tea parties for she is a follower of the way of tea, *chado*, in which tea is used to help one contemplate higher ideals and not serve as an occasion for gossip and laughter. Still everything must be perfect. I have written my commands for the tea sweets to be delivered directly by Keiko to the pastry chef. I have fretted endlessly over the right sweet to serve and then it came to me in the middle of the night — *hanagoromo*. *Hanagoromo* means "flowering robe," and it is, in fact, the sweet for this early part of the month of March. It is filled with the fragrant adzuki beans and then folded into a skin of pink pastry that billows like the sleeve of a kimono.

I am very excited. If things go well when I give this tea, Tomaki will tell the Prince how grown up I have become, despite my shortness. I know the *waka* that I have composed is not perfect, but it has all the ingredients Auntie says a good *waka* must have: something about the seasons, a sense of quiet, and an underlying feeling of mystery. I think I am not so good with the mystery part.

Yayoi March 7, 1858

I have pondered that word "mystery" now. Little did I realize when I wrote the poem just before my tea party that it would come to have such meaning. But it has, and it has nothing to do with my *waka*. I think it has to do with me. I think I might be at the center, or part of a great mystery. But I must tell my story in order.

My tea party was perfect. Except now that seems almost meaningless. Auntie and Mother and Lady Tomaki, who is the most beautiful and elegant lady I have ever met, each brought a *waka* of their own. Their hair was newly waxed and their teeth freshly blackened. I cannot wait to be old enough to blacken my teeth with the iron powder. I think it adds so much to a woman's smile. Lady Tomaki's is so beautiful. Some say she is a great writer, as good as Lady Murasaki who wrote *The Tale of Genji*, which chronicles the adventures of the man known as the "Shining Prince" of the medieval court. I am not yet permitted to read of Genji's amorous adventures. So I cannot compare the writing. But all the ladies were very complimentary of my *waka* and very impressed with the tea and the sweets.

The maids brought in our spring kimonos for viewing. There was much chatter about how weary we are of the plum-blossom colors of winter, and all the winter designs that we wear from November through February. And as the maids spread out the kimonos, we welcomed back the colors, the prints with the blossoms of spring like old friends. For only now may we begin to wear them.

But during the tea party, I was feeling all the while that this talk of silks and color and painted blossoms covered up something. It is what was not being said that was perhaps the most disturbing. I felt that these women knew something that I do not. I saw it in the way that Auntie kept clutching her hands and rubbing her swollen knuckles. There was a shrillness to Lady Tomaki's laughter that seemed not quite natural, and my mother swallowed, not when she was eating, but, in a way that one might gulp down a fear rather than a pastry. And there was absolutely no talk of the Prince, my future husband. It was so obvious to me that I dared not ask about him. I began to think that perhaps he is very sick or maybe even dead.

Then Keiko brought out a beautiful kimono that belonged to my mother when she was just my age. It was a very pale yellow with a pattern of willow leaves in a haunting silvery green. Every year I dream that I might be tall enough to wear this kimono. So I tried it on. It fell in such deep folds around my ankles that there was no way the sash, the obi, could have been tied properly to ever hold it up. I was so sad and then, perhaps distracted by my disappointment I just blurted out, "How tall is Prince Arisugawa now?"

"Oh, very short, very short," my mother said quickly. "Short for a boy who is so much older than you."

"Unbecomingly short," Lady Tomaki said, and then they both looked pointedly at Auntie in some kind of expectation. Auntie seemed caught off guard but then quickly recovered. "Short," she blurted out the word. "Yes, very short."

And here the mystery began. I could not believe it, but for the next five minutes they spoke of nothing else but how unattractively short the Prince was. How it was delicate and lovely for a woman to be so small, but a man must be larger. And I kept thinking, *He still might grow.* So I said so, and then they all said, "Oh, no. All the men in that family are short." And they looked at Lady Tomaki because she is related to the family, and she nodded sagely that yes, this was so.

I am very confused. Why do they say such things about the boy I am supposed to marry? So neither of us are ever to grow? What does it matter? I like Arisugawa, short or tall. He is funny, short or tall. I wrote another poem.

> *My Prince is too short*
> *as is my kimono*
> *too long*

I sent this to my mother.

Yayoi March 8, 1858

The mystery deepens. There is not yet an answer from my mother to the *waka* that I sent to her. That is not really proper. When one person sends a poem to another, the other is supposed to respond with a poetic answer.

Dare I send one to Lady Tomaki?

Later

Yes, I do. Here it is:

> So short you say
> And yet you go to great lengths to say it
> The cherry blossom pruned in winter sprouts in spring

Two hours later

I cannot believe it. Lady Tomaki's maid has just delivered this response to me from her lady.

> Cherry blossoms fallen still give scent
> And on the petals sparrows
> wipe their muddy feet

I am completely confused now. Although I think that Lady Tomaki understands that Prince Arisugawa is still attractive to me, for she says the blossoms still give scent. But then there are the words of the sparrows with the muddy feet who dirty the blossom petals. Who is the sparrow? Me? The court ladies maybe? The Emperor's mother? There is something frightening here.

Perhaps I shall learn more in two days. There is to be a

banquet to celebrate the changeover to our spring kimonos. A Noh play shall be performed.

Yayoi March 12, 1858

Well, it was a very strange celebration. It began with a viewing of the cherry blossoms in the garden of the new pavilion, the one my brother built especially for his little son, Prince Sachi-no-miya. He will do anything for that child. I suppose it is because he is the only child of the Emperor who has lived beyond the age of four. He is now almost six. All the noble court ladies were there including Lady Nakayama Yoshiko, who is Sachi's mother and the Emperor's favorite *nyogo*, at least until Lady Tomaki arrived.

So this was the first thing I noticed: many grim-faced ladies whose demeanors did not match the light, airy beauty of their spring kimonos. Indeed, Auntie, upon seeing them all lined up, muttered a spontaneous poem that nearly made me laugh:

Cherry blossoms fade
Shedding petals like tears
As court ladies redden and fury rises

The women all looked rather tortured with their painted lips pressed together into small red slashes, and their plucked eyebrows as thin as minnows colliding into frowns. Everyone pretended to look at the cherry blossoms but no one really did. They were stealing glances at the Emperor, who did not even pretend to look at the blossoms. He had eyes only for Lady Tomaki. And indeed, many of the women, as they stood on the viewing platform, were reddening under their rice powder with anger or perhaps fear or I do not know what. And then just when I thought the tension would become unbearable, little Sachi went tearing across the garden with his bamboo sword crying, "Kill the white-faced devils!" Well, his bad behavior was astonishing in this garden of supposedly perfect serenity and fragile beauty. The spell was broken. The Emperor clapped his hands in delight, swooped down from the viewing platform, and scooped up his son in his arms.

There are more than three hundred ladies in the royal court, and all of them in one way or another are charged with the well-being of Sachi. They decide what he wears, eats, when he goes to bed, and whom he can or cannot see. But right then, they all stood powerless as the Emperor swung him up onto his shoulders in a most undignified way. But it saved the kimono banquet celebration. It broke the tension. Not to say, however, that everything was exactly normal.

There were, throughout the evening, many side-glances that darted toward Lady Tomaki. I thought nothing of this really until little Sachi demanded that I sit by him at one point during the long evening meal. I am one of the few people allowed this privilege. So I found myself sitting next to the little boy and the Emperor's mother. As one might imagine, the Empress Mother is not overly fond of the court ladies who become mistresses of her son, and since my mother was once the mistress to her own husband, the previous Emperor, she never passes up an opportunity to say something slightly insulting about my mother. She often refers to my mother as having "peculiar country ways." It is true that my mother was the daughter of a samurai who had a large farm in the north, but this hardly makes her a peasant. Nonetheless, the Empress Mother has always been civil to me. And on this evening she was as well. But suddenly she turned to the lady next to her and in a whisper loud enough for me to hear, she said, "I do hope no children come from this liaison of the Lady Tomaki and my son. It is well known that the children tend to be weak, slight of stature. Yes, they say Prince Arisugawa is quite pathetic in appearance."

At that moment I thought of the sparrows in Lady

Tomaki's poem. Was I sitting next to the sparrow who wiped its muddy feet on the fallen cherry blossoms? I did not understand this at all. My mother and Auntie also spoke poorly of this dear, young Prince whom I am to marry and whom I do believe I love. Why are they all against me? Usually, they are against one another: The Empress Mother against my mother. The Emperor's wife against the newest *nyogo* who catches the Emperor's eye. There are many sides to these court intrigues. But everyone is on the same side now except me. I began the evening thinking they were all angry and indignant over Lady Tomaki. But why me now?

A special serving lady for Sachi came with a platter of river trout sliced as thin as paper. She wore a cotton mask over her mouth as all who serve the little Prince must do, so he will not catch their germs when being served food. He also eats with extra-long chopsticks, which is felt to further protect him. Another masked lady came and then I looked around and it seemed to me that in a strange manner everyone there was wearing a mask. I was suddenly transported into a weird and alien world. I thought I knew nothing before. Now I know less. I do not even recognize the expression on my dear auntie's face as she observed me with her stony eyes buried in the creases of her old face. And oddly enough, I felt closer to the Noh actors in the play who, indeed, perform with masks. At least in the play one knows who the demons are. And despite the mask, expressions can change just by the manner in which an actor turns his head and allows the light to fall. The Noh masks can become faces with skin and muscle and feeling. But not the masks that the court wore this evening.

Yayoi March 15, 1858
The Time That the Frog Eggs Begin to Float

I do not know how to ask Auntie about this problem. I do not know what words to say. But something has changed here. Yes, I know that my brother the Emperor is upset about the treaty and the shogun who has great powers and has let in the barbarians from America. But what does that have to do with me? And yet I feel that somehow my fate is tied to those white devils.

I went for a walk by myself in the gardens. I saw the eggs of the frogs floating in clumps like clear, little, glass beads.

No more poems from Lady Tomaki. None from my mother. And Auntie is no help at all, anyway. This is the season for the *kami*, the ghosts. Auntie is so superstitious.

She thinks there is a ghost lurking in every cupboard. She consults constantly with the astrological charts. She was supposed to visit a cousin the other day outside the palace but would not go when she realized she would have to travel in a southeasterly direction across Kyoto to reach her cousin's house. How silly!

During this time of the year and then again in autumn, Auntie lets the *kami* run her life. I know there are *kami* about, but I do not think they are as powerful or move around as quickly or even pay that much attention to one single person. Besides, I don't need invisible spirits causing problems for me. The Emperor's mother looks slyly at me, and my own mother was not invited to the moon-viewing ceremony held last evening in the garden of the ponds. These are problems enough and have nothing to do with *kami*.

Yayoi March 16, 1858
The Time When the Black Dots Grow in the Frog Eggs

Not once during the time of the full moon has my mother or my auntie been invited to the moon-viewing platform. I am invited but I do not go because I find it insulting that they do not invite those closest to me. But tomorrow night I am ordered to go. And what's more, the Empress Kujo's hairdresser has been ordered to dress my hair. She comes today. This hairdressing will take hours and means I must sleep on a drum pillow tonight so my hair will not be disturbed. Sleeping on a drum pillow is awful. One simply does not sleep, for the hard wood drum with its concave sides is arranged under one's neck. Auntie says I must not complain. I must be grown up about this. She waves her hand as if my words are gnats. Then goes off to chase a ghost.

Later

I cannot sleep. So I might as well write. First, I must dress Heian style for the moon viewing. This style is from the old classical period and one must wear six layers of robes. In the real Heian times, the women might wear as many as eighteen layers! I wear the colors of earliest spring, shades of wisteria, and the outermost kimono is lavender, lined with blue. But this is all very odd. Usually, a girl does not dress this way until she has had her teeth-blackening ceremony. And I have not. The only other time is perhaps at a wedding or possibly to meet her future husband at the betrothal ceremony. Well, I already had mine when I was four. So I don't understand why I am required to wear this style now.

It took six hours to dress my hair. First, the comb girl prepared my hair. This always takes the longest, for my hair reaches to just below my knees and by the time I am the age of my mother, I shall be able to step on it. For like all Japanese girls and ladies, we never cut it. Perhaps the only thing good about being old is that when you get as old as Auntie, one's hair starts to break off so it takes less time to comb it. Then Sayuri, the main hairdresser, began to crease the hair with the hot tongs that have been heated on the hibachi. Sayuri is a bad-tempered little crone, and she is always yelling at the girl who prepares the hibachi that the coals are too hot or too cold. She began to dress my hair. I felt my very body was being manipulated in a way that seemed strange. I don't know why, but suddenly it was as if a little demon inhabited me and I just blurted out, "Why not fashion my hair into a *Shimoda* chignon?" I love twisted knots of hair but no court ladies ever wear their hair knotted in this fashion. I thought perhaps Sayuri would have a heart attack when she heard my words. Indeed, she screeched like a screech owl. Then yammered at me. What did I think I was . . . one of those harlots from the Floating World, serving tea in a teahouse, showing my elbows? I could see that her assistants were barely containing their laughter.

She pushed my head roughly and complained that I was not bending it down properly. "Your Grace." She scowled. "This is the most important part of the hairstyle, and the Emperor wants you to look suitable."

"Suitable for what?" I asked. "Suitable for the moon?" Her two assistants giggled out loud at this and she turned and hissed at them just like a snake. They clamped their mouths shut. I could not wait until it was all over.

Yayoi March 17, 1858

So now I know! The mystery has been solved. I have not had my hair waxed and combed for the moon. No, it was for Tokugawa Yoshitomi from the distinguished Kii family of Wakayama. He is just my age, and it is said that he is to be the next shogun of Japan. He was at the moon viewing with Lord Naosuke. Some say Lord Naosuke is more powerful than the present shogun, who is ailing. I would have had to have a head made of wood not to see what was happening. The court ladies who looked slyly at me two days ago were all smiles now. The Emperor greeted me very warmly, and I was given the best seat next to him on the moon-viewing platform. Next to me, they seated this boy, Yoshitomi. The court ladies did what they did best — made small talk to bring about a conversation between me and the boy. But the talk, of course, could never be natural. It was all so . . . so arranged, and I think Yoshitomi realized this as much as I did. We remained stiff and distant as if we were wooden puppets with our parts worked by different puppet masters.

But this was the strangest. Others, too, were puppets, and I saw the Empress Mother, that evil woman, lean over and whisper something to the Empress Kujo. Kujo started as if she had forgotten something and then said in a very stilted voice, "Oh, yes, and in a very few months our dear Chikako shall have her first teeth-blackening ceremony."

Well, I was shocked. It is only a girl's mother who announces such news. It is very improper for anyone else to do so. Kujo is not my mother. This was a terrible insult to my mother and my late father. I was simply furious and could not speak a word after that. As soon as the moon viewing was over, I rushed back to my apartments through an autumn garden, for I knew no one would go this way.

I was wrong. One person did go this way, following me. Lady Tomaki. My rice powder was streaked with tears. "How could they take that away from me and Mother and Auntie?"

I cried when Tomaki first caught up with me. "I don't understand. Teeth-blackening is as important as chopstick ceremony or first hair ceremony."

I began breathlessly listing all the dozens of ceremonies that mark a person's passage from babyhood through childhood until their wedding. All such ceremonies are planned and their dates decided by a child's mother and father in consultation, of course, with astrologers. But the first time a young girl has her teeth blackened is especially important for the mother to decide.

"The next thing they will do is decide to change my birthday again!" I blurted out. And as soon as I said it I knew it was true or at least a possibility. A birthday is sometimes changed to make it more harmonious with one's future mate. My original birthday was already harmonious with that of Arisugawa's astrological signs. When they changed it to escape the year of the Fire Horse, they made sure that it would still be harmonious with Arisugawa's.

"I won't! I won't! I won't change my birthday!" I stamped my foot as the moon slid down the black back of the night. "It is my birthday. It is my birthday!" It was so perfectly clear now. They were arranging for me to marry this Yoshitomi of the shogunate family of Tokugawa. Therefore, my birthday would be changed to be agreeable with the birthday of the new husband they had picked for me.

Lady Tomaki tried to calm me down. But the more she said, the angrier I got. It was all part of a plan, she explained, a secret plan for Yoshitomi to be the next shogun. And if this were to happen it would strengthen the position of Emperor Komei, especially if the new shogun was married to the Emperor's sister, a Princess. Yoshitomi was backed by the very lords who agreed with my brother that the treaty should never have been made with the Americans. Lady Tomaki explained that they were part of the group that revered the Emperor and wanted to throw out the barbarous white devils. "Now, do you not want that?" Tomaki asked.

"But my brother the Emperor is already revered. He is a descendent of the sun goddess," I said.

Lady Tomaki blinked and looked steadily at me. "As a God he can do nothing. But as a man he will have power. Do you not want that?" she repeated.

It might sound silly, but what I really wanted was my own birthday. So I said nothing and stomped off in angry silence. Indeed, do what they might, the Fire Horse was rising within me. I felt its heat.

Yayoi March 21, 1858
The Time When the Day Grows Even with the Night

Auntie Umi sleeps with a *kayari* dish burning. Is that not silly? There are no mosquitoes this time of year, but she blends the sawdust of the nutmeg tree with special powders to drive away not insects, but ghosts. A year ago I would have thought it was silly, too. But now I believe that the *kami* chase me in this month of spring as much as the mosquitoes chase me in the summer. Auntie of all people always wanted the Prince and me to marry. Even when they spoke of him being short and ugly she could hardly bring herself to say such words. She is as sad as I am, and she believes ghosts cause my problems. I could tell right away that Yoshitomi is different from Prince Arisugawa. And I know that Auntie could see this as well.

I don't feel like doing anything and usually this is my favorite time of year. I have not even gone to the garden of the ponds. The frog eggs have hatched by now, and the tadpoles must be swimming. I used to delight in watching them. I would concentrate so hard that I could almost watch their tails disappear. There is a time when the tadpoles' legs begin to form and one can see them all curled up under the skin and, then if one is patient, she might catch the moment when they first break through. It is a wonderful mystery to me. Imagine within the space of a few days being able to grow another body part that would take you into another part of this world. Before that, the tadpole could only swim and live in the water, and after, it could hop and leap and breathe air of the world above. I know I am not the first person to dream of flight, but suppose human beings could live in two worlds, suppose buried deep in our shoulders were the bones of wings and we could fly away. Fly away. That is what I dream of. If I could fly away from this palace called heaven.

That is why I do not go to the garden of the ponds — because I envy the tadpoles, the mystery of their transformation, and the promise of their new life.

Uzuki April 1, 1858

So the only changes I observe are the ones inside. The hanging kettle in the teahouse used all winter and early spring is now exchanged for the one that sets directly on the coals of the sunken hearth. The big fires need not burn now, and the guests do not need the heat of such a fire.

Uzuki April 3, 1858
The Time the Paulwonia Blossoms Open

And they do! Outside my window. And that is always a sign that it is time for hair-washing day. Auntie instructed Keiko to prepare the cauldrons of white water, *shioromizu*. So she soaked pailfuls of rice for two hours in the cauldrons. Extra maids were called in to help us. Auntie's hair, although broken off, is still long — much longer than she stands tall. Mine is just below the back of my knees and will, by the time I marry, be to the floor. But then again who knows when or whom I shall marry these days?

After our hair was washed, our maids combed and combed and combed it. For hours, Auntie and Mother and I sat near the charcoal brazier while the maids combed, for there was a bit of chill in the air. Mother's hair has not broken off, but is long and healthy, and her servant must back out the door to comb it completely. The maids put almond oil on their combs and a pleasant scent rose in the air. Then just before the last combing, we all stood with our hair draping over a special incense burner and its sweet fragrance rose and mixed in with the almond oil. We all smelled so good by the end of hair-washing day.

Uzuki April 5, 1858
The Time of Pure Brightness

In the old Chinese calendar, they call these days the time of pure brightness. For this is when the air is most clear and the light is like transparent silver, and yet for me it seems like a time of shadows and darkness. My mother and Auntie worry because I don't eat. I have indeed grown thinner. I must tie my sash tighter. I seem to shrink in my robes. It is not just that I miss the Prince whom I realize I hardly know. It is not even that it has been decided that I shall marry the boy Yoshitomi, but it is that I am a pawn in this game of the Emperor's and the shogunate. I know that I have no say about my life, but must they take away my very birthday? What is to be left that is just me — pure me? I dream that someday I shall wake up and not even know myself. I shall stand before a looking glass and say, "Who is this?" and then feel a dim longing for someone that I vaguely remember.

Uzuki April 10, 1858
The Time of the Rain to Coax the Rice

Lady Tomaki entertained us at tea. They tried very hard to tempt me with the seasonal sweets, for everyone talks about how thin I grow. One would think that is all there was to talk about. But the more they talked, the less hungry I grew. You see, I am even more worried as the palace is overrun with men from the *nijo*, the shogun's castle here in Kyoto, including the higher-ups from the shogun's government, the *bakufu*. There is much talk that the present shogun, Iesada, is near death. The Emperor seems happy, not that Iesada is near death, but that he, the Emperor, is being paid attention — attention and not just reverence. Perhaps he is becoming less of a God and more of a man. Lady Tomaki hinted at this at tea. She giggled and turned pink under her rice powder and hid her reddening face behind her fan, which she fluttered madly. "Oh, he is a man!" she said.

The court ladies at this tea were the ones who like Lady Tomaki, so she need not fear their jealousy or their loyalty. There was much talk about the Shining Prince, Genji, from the Lady Murasaki Shibuki's book — the book that I am not permitted to read until I have had my teeth-blackening ceremony. So I found this tea rather boring even though one of my favorite seasonal sweets, *hanaikada*, or raft with cherry blossoms, was served. It has a filling smooth as silk, and the cherry flavor is so delicate one can taste the perfume long after swallowing. Still I was not hungry and merely picked at mine. While the other ladies were giggling and talking about *The Tale of Genji*, Auntie watched me closely.

Uzuki April 15, 1858

Indeed, my birthday is to be changed. So I am to be born for the third time in my short life. But it feels like death. What is left of me? Would my brother and the court be fearful if I told them that the Fire Horse still stirs deep inside me? That in spite of all, that is what is left that is truly me — the ghost of the Fire Horse.

Uzuki April 16, 1858

If one more person tries to make me eat I shall scream.

Later

My mouth was set to scream when Auntie walked in but she talked not of food. She first asked me about my dreams. And as a matter of fact, I did have one last night. I dreamed of thunder and climbing a mountain. Auntie clapped her hands in glee. A smile broke over her face. "Double good omen!" she pronounced. I knew that hearing thunder in one's dreams is good, but I didn't realize that climbing a mountain was as well.

"Quick!" she said and bid me to put on my plainest kimono, the one with the shafts of winter wheat. I gasped. Not even seasonal. Only the poor people would dare dress so. She bid me to put over it a *michiyuki* cloak. "We are going on the road?" I asked. For this, in fact, is the real and literal meaning of the word *michiyuki. But it is too warm,* I thought and then I realized that she did not want anyone to see me in this winter kimono. "Where are we going?"

"Kennin-ji," Auntie replied.

I was somewhat stunned. This is one of the city's oldest Zen Buddhist temples, but to get there we shall have to travel in an unlucky direction on this day of the calendar. And for Auntie to do this was unbelievable. I do not believe in *kami*, but Auntie does and to travel in an unlucky direction can mean that there might be *kami* waiting for one at every turn.

"Quick!" she hissed. "I have ordered a palanquin. We go now."

❀

Midnight

The frogs do peep
Their sounds fall into the night
Like dewdrops on my ears

Yes, now I hear the frogs at last. And I have eaten the seasonal delights, the *hanakaida*, the raft with cherry blossoms, the bounteous flowers made from candied fruits, and now a small mountain of soba noodles, and a bowl of miso soup. Yes, I eat. I hear. I feel, for all my senses have been awakened. I have seen Arisugawa at the temple of Kennin-ji. And he is not short, nor ugly, nor sickly. Indeed he is my "Shining Prince." My Genji. And whom do I have to thank for all this? None other than my romantic old Auntie Umi. But I am tired now and must rest. I shall write more tomorrow.

Uzuki April 17, 1858

Now for my story. I suppose I should have been suspicious from the start when Auntie told me to wear my kimono with the shafts of winter wheat, and then my traveling robe over that on such a hot day. But I really did not suspect anything until she turned to Keiko and said,

"Keiko, you understand, do you not, why you shall not be going?"

Keiko bowed low. "Yes, honorable Tanaka Umiyaki," she said, using my auntie's full name. I was completely baffled. I have never gone outside the palace gates without my maids. "And your brother, Matsui, is waiting. All is arranged?"

"Yes," she bowed again.

I was mystified. Matsui, Keiko's brother, did odd jobs around the palace grounds and was known for his strength, but he had no real rank and would never be engaged to carry the palanquin of court ladies of rank and certainly not an Imperial Princess.

But Auntie Umi made up some nonsense that she told me and Keiko about how a maid of my mother's was coming instead. But this was not so. When we met Matsui, there was a double palanquin waiting for us, not at the Gishumon gate, through which Princes and Princesses and royal peers enter, nor did we go to the Sakuheimon gate in the north wall that is used by consorts and ladies-in-waiting. Instead, we went to the Seishomon gate, which is used by the most ordinary visitors who have applied for permission to enter the palace grounds for one reason or another. Our palanquin was waiting with four bearers.

"Bend your head down and grab my arm as if you are

helping me to walk." Now I knew something was very strange because to reach this gate from our apartments, one had to travel paths that led in a northeasterly direction — a most unlucky direction. It is so unlucky that even the outer wall of the palace was built without a northeast corner. So for this temple expedition we were required to travel in two unlucky directions. And with no maids! I could not imagine what had happened to Auntie. Maybe she was going crazy. But I climbed into the palanquin and she sat beside me. She clutched my hand in a fierce grip as the bearers lifted our curtained cage.

The bearers trotted along smoothly, although we could not be much of a burden to them. Together, Auntie and I probably weigh no more than a family's yearly rice bag. From the noise outside and the smells, I could tell that we had left the palace behind and that we were no longer in the Imperial park. I heard the clamor of the vendors, the braying of a donkey, and the smell of fish cooking, and greasy noodles. Then every once in a while, winding through the air like a ribbon of sweetness, there was the smell of one of the sweet shops for which our city is famous. And to go to this temple, we cut straight through the Gion, which we never do when we are in one of the Imperial palanquins. The Gion is part of what is known as the Floating World. It is where many of the geishas live. It is considered quite bawdy. No Princess would ever travel through it. But I was a disguised Princess today in my gown of winter wheat. So I peeked. I saw what I think was a geisha. She wore an obi, a long, sweeping sash around her kimono, and her hair was arranged in a style they call the split peach, which is considered quite vulgar — at least Auntie says so. I soon spotted another. This one carried a lovely oiled-paper umbrella with lotus blossoms.

All the time we traveled, Auntie clutched my hand, her fingernails digging into my skin. Her eyes were clamped shut. And her lips moved in a silent whisper around the words of the Lotus sutra, one of the sacred texts of the Buddha. She was as frightened as I have ever seen her. And yet I did not understand why — until we got to the temple. An old nun greeted us as we climbed from the palanquin, crossed a small bridge, and entered the temple grounds through a big black gate. Auntie had purchased two lotus blossoms from the nuns at the entrance, and we made a *puja*, an offering to the Buddha. She began to recite a vow in which she promised that if she were to gain complete enlightenment, she would dedicate her knowledge to all people who hear her name so they might also gain. This is a very serious vow. I could not imagine what Auntie was up to. I knew that she is a devout Buddhist and she speaks often of retreating to a temple and becoming a Buddhist nun. When our meditation and prayers were finished, Auntie rose and motioned for me to follow her.

We began walking toward the garden of the pond. The sun was out, and the golden carp in the water looked like licks of flame under the surface as they darted about. The willow trees and the cherry blossoms conspired to weave a brocade for spring. We were going to the teahouse on the east side of the pond. Tea is a very important part of the temple of Kennin-ji. But this taking of tea was nothing like the parties that I have written about in my diary. There is no gossip. There is lovely ritual that helps one meditate and free one's mind. This kind of tea ceremony is called *chanoyu*. Now, imagine my surprise when we arrived in the waiting room and I noticed a striking-looking young man. It was Prince Arisugawa!

Before I could recover myself, the *hanto*, or assistant to the tea master, led us to the dew ground, a small garden where we sprinkled our hands and rid ourselves of the dust of the road. My hands trembled like leaves in a cold wind as I rinsed them. I prayed that I would not fall over into the stone basin. Finally, we were led into the tearoom through the sliding *shoji* screens. And then the next surprise. We were welcomed by our host.

I was not sure of the meaning of all this, but I felt Auntie next to me and her hand lightly touched mine. She looked at the scroll that hangs in the alcove. There is no other decoration except for flowers and this specially selected scroll. On the scroll is a Buddhist scripture by the poet Kyoroku.

Above the mountain's snow-white vapor floats
An airy voice: the skylark's rising notes.

In addition to the scroll, there was one other decoration in the tearoom. A bamboo basket containing one small branch of roses. It was a kind of rose that grows wild on the riverbanks. Everyone knows the story of how this rose came to grow. A young woman and a young man who were in love were forced apart, and before they parted they looked at their reflections in a mirror. They then together buried the mirror along a riverbank and later the roses grew there. It was at this moment of looking at the rose that the significance of this story stole into our hearts and minds, and Arisugawa and I looked up at each other and smiled. The rest of the ceremony was something of a blur to me.

It all tasted wonderful and the sweetness in my mouth mingled with the sweet face of this Prince. Auntie and the tea master carried on the conversation. Thank heavens. There are things one is supposed to say at certain times. One must comment on the tea or the shape of the kettle, or perhaps recite a classic *waka*. I cannot remember if I did any of this.

I am too tired now to write more. But I feel at peace, and Auntie promises me that we shall all meet again.

Satsuki May 2, 1858
The Time the Hoopoe Bird Descends to the Mulberry

Time passes so quickly now. Arisugawa and I have exchanged many *waka* poems through secret messengers with whom Auntie has contacts. And once more, we have met at Kennin-ji for tea. I must always wear my dullest kimonos to escape from here, and yesterday I did complain to Arisugawa that I was so sorry I could not wear the one with the peonies, which are almost ready to bloom in the garden. So today I received this poem from him:

> *Winter wheat*
> *Gathers the bloom of the peony*
> *Upon occasion*

My heart nearly stopped when I read these lines. I am so happy, and now I grow plump again and mind not that there is another moon viewing soon and that Tokugawa Yoshitomi, the boy that they all have their hopes set on for me, shall be present. I tuck deep in my heart and my mind's eye the image of Arisugawa and, like the mirror buried at the riverbank, it makes me bloom inside.

Satsuki May 5, 1858
The Time That the Peonies Show Pink

Today was *Tango No Sekku*, or Boys' Day Celebration. Of course, here in the palace one would have thought that there was only one boy in the entire country, and that boy is Sachi. Silk banners with Sachi's Imperial crest flew from every roof of the palace. There was a huge display of miniature helmets and toy swords and the little samurai warrior dolls. Indeed, this holiday is said to go back to the great samurai victories in a time of civil war. It seems to me that it is an excuse for little boys to behave badly. And Sachi certainly outdid himself, screeching, throwing tantrums if he did not get his way, waving his toy sword and threatening one nurse with instant decapitation — a favorite samurai method of punishing a person for the least infraction. Of course, all the noblemen who were filled with *shobu-sake*, a kind of potent drink made from the leaves of iris, thought him quite winning. The best parts of Boys' Day, as far as I am concerned, are two: One is the special sweets, which are wrapped in bamboo leaves and called *chimaki*; the second is the fragrant iris baths we take. Mother, Auntie, Lady Tomaki, and I all climbed into the *ofuro* together and soaked for nearly an hour.

Satsuki May 8, 1858
The Time That the Rice Sprouts

Once more I must submit to the hot tongs and wax and comb of Sayuri. Once more I must wear six layers of robes. They hang now above the incense burner to make them fragrant. Auntie comes in and dismisses Keiko in the middle of her dressing me.

"Now you remember your own Shining Prince and do not let their talk disturb you." This is significant. Although she arranges the meetings with Arisugawa, Auntie has never directly spoken to me about why she is doing this. As in Japanese paintings, in which what is not painted becomes in its absence as important as what is painted, what has been left unsaid about Arisugawa is as important as what is said about Yoshitomi and the Emperor's plans. Now, indeed, it does worry me that she should so much as mention it.

She smiled quickly and said, "And tomorrow I have a surprise for you. So no matter what happens tonight know that tomorrow shall be wonderful."

Later

It better be wonderful! Yoshitomi was the least of my problems tonight. The Empress Mother and Nakayama Yoshiko, chief consort, seemed to be looking daggers at all of us — by *us*, I mean Auntie, my mother, and most of all Lady Tomaki. I am very worried. I must say it was very difficult to concentrate on the moon. The Empress Mother is, I think, no, *I know*, a very strange woman. She loves cats, of which there are many throughout the palace. They are, indeed, the favorite Imperial pet. Although I myself am not such a cat lover. But the Empress Mother is mad for them. She always has two or three on her lap — even while she eats. There is her favorite, Hiroki, a huge, disgusting, fat thing, all white except for one splotch of black over its left eye. Last week, she elevated this stupid fat cat to an Imperial ranking! Some say my brother agreed to let his mother do this if he could keep Lady Tomaki as his number one *nyogo*. There is much idle and often vicious talk in this court. One hardly knows what to believe. But it is true that the cat now has a rank. And it sat there on her lap throughout the entire banquet!

It was a moon banquet with the traditional rice-and-sweet-bean dumplings. One of the court ladies made a remark about Lady Tomaki hiding her dumplings and everyone giggled, except me. I didn't understand. The Empress Mother turned red with fury. Yoshitomi was perfectly nice, but so dull. He tried to come up with poems at the appropriate moments, for instance as a cloud slid across the moon. I could tell he had been waiting for this one moment all night and had probably worked on the poem for days. But it just plopped. That is the only word I can think to describe it. Here is his poem:

> *Cloud across moon*
> *Goes whoosh*
> *Bye Bye Bye*

Is that terrible or not?

Satsuki May 9, 1858
The Time That the Cucumbers Flourish

The noble lady who made the dumpling joke about Lady Tomaki has been banished. The court is in an uproar. I did not find out any of this until Auntie and I had returned from our secret outing. And, as she promised, it was wonderful. I cannot believe it but we went to a sumo tournament. And Arisugawa was there! I have only seen the sumo matches held here on the palace grounds. It is much different in public. They fight rougher, I believe, and they have many more fouls counted against them for pulling hair and eye gouging, which is strictly forbidden. And the *rikishi*, the wrestlers, seemed even bigger. Auntie is very devoted to sumo, and I think that is why we went, because her favorite wrestler, Mashimoto, was wrestling. I think this man must weigh four hundred pounds, at least. I shall never forget the first smack when their bellies collided. And then within seconds the match was over! Mashimoto won.

Auntie told Arisugawa and me something interesting. She said that he won not because he weighed more, because in fact he did not, but that he won because of his concentration. She says Mashimoto's stare is as powerful as his body. And she is right. At the beginning of a match, salt is scattered in the ring to purify the ground in accordance with an ancient tradition. The wrestlers crouch with their fists planted on the ground and stare into each other's eyes. During this staring part, they begin to slap each other's faces very rapidly, so rapidly their hands seem to blur and this is their attempt to break each other's stare of concentration, but Mashimoto's stare never breaks. Much of sumo is mental warfare. Auntie says that the best sumo wrestlers, like Mashimoto, often win the match before the first move is even made. She says that despite their immense size, this is a mental game more than a physical one. Then she turned to me and Arisugawa and said, "Much of life is that way, my children."

I think I am learning many lessons from Auntie beyond those of brush painting and poetry, or the music lessons that my *koto* teacher gives me. These are delicate and subtle lessons. Auntie is preparing me for something, but I am not quite sure what. At first, I thought that Auntie was just a foolish old romantic consumed with planning meetings between Arisugawa and myself. But now I am thinking that it is more. I think I shall make a list here of these lessons.

Lesson #1) The lesson of the *omokage* rose and the story of the mirror: A memory cannot be destroyed but lives on in love.

Lesson #2) The lesson of the two mountain peaks linked by mists: They rise through the vapors over the valley forever, through passing seasons. Mountains endure as seasons change.

Lesson #3) The lesson of the sumo wrestlers: Size is not everything. Mental concentration is equally important.

Satsuki May 10, 1858

So far, the official changing of my birth date has not been made. So today is my birthday — of course, not my real birthday, which is August 1, but the date to which it was first changed when I was still an infant. We had a small party. Lady Tomaki came for tea and so did my brother the Emperor. Lady Tomaki gave me a writing case, because this one shall be full before the end of the year. The Emperor honored me with a doll that had belonged to our father's mother.

Later

I have received this perfect poem from Arisugawa for my birthday:

Like Paulwonia blossoms
drifting down from the trees
so my thoughts turn to you

If Auntie read this, she would commend his excellent sensitivities. He has included all a birthday poem should: First and most important, it is an affirmation to me that this indeed is my birthday, on the edge of summer, for the Paulwonia only blooms then. So my birthday cannot be changed by Empress Mother or anyone. Second, he has made a connection through nature to him. I am a source of happiness for him. And all of these thoughts are folded into the elements of the season.

Satsuki May 14, 1858

Well, the Empress Mother grows crazier every day. As if elevating her cat to an Imperial rank wasn't enough madness, she has had a court painter paint a net on the painting of the carp. She claims that they swim out of the picture at night and into the garden pool by her apartments and the cats get overly excited with the fish leaping in the pond. She cannot sleep for the racket. My mother says that this is all caused by the Empress

Mother's resentment that the Sento gosho, the palace for the retired Emperor and his wife, was not rebuilt after the last fire, and she feels very cheated. Therefore, she tries all sorts of sly little tricks and schemes to keep the workmen and artisans busy on her present apartments. If she cannot have her own palace she will create the next best thing. She is truly a horrible woman. No wonder my father preferred my mother to her.

Satsuki May 16, 1858

There was a tea ceremony yesterday, in the garden of the ponds, in honor of the memory of Shuko, a renowned old master of the tea from many hundreds of years ago. Although I suppose the perfect scroll had been selected — summer boats on a river, and the blossoms in the vase were that of the mandarin orange tree that blooms now in earliest summer — and even the poem was perfect, I felt an emptiness. Yoshitomi was back and in attendance. I was seated next to him, and he was next to the Emperor's chamberlain, Iwakura Tomomi, who is a very powerful man. He has sly and cunning ways, and it disturbed me to see him sitting so close to Yoshitomi and whispering to him. This is very poor form. I could tell that Auntie was furious. It has long been Auntie's complaint that here in the court, the tea ceremony has degenerated into a shameless circus. That, of course, is an exaggeration. But the rules are often broken and the spirit, the *wabi*, is broken as well. The *wabi* is a notion of beauty, a beauty and order that exist beneath the surface of things, which is the heart of tea ceremony. It was sadly missing here as court ladies looked slyly at Tomaki and everyone seemed to try to push Yoshitomi and me together at every opportunity. It became very awkward, especially those times between the first part of tea ceremony, when the light meal is served, and the second part, when tea is prepared. Between these two acts of the ceremony, we are to retire to the tea garden, the *roji*, and wait. Everyone proceeded to stare at Yoshitomi and me. I would have much preferred to look at the peonies, which were almost in full bloom and, indeed, I did wear my peony kimono, and yet I felt dull next to this boy. As dull as winter wheat. I caught, from the corner of my eye, Iwakui Tomomi giving him a signal and then, like one of little Sachi's wind-up toys, Yoshitomi recited a poem. But it was the wrong one!

> *A lovely thing to see:*
> *Through the paper window's hole,*
> *The galaxy*

It was a famous summer-night poem by the ancient master Issa. They must have told Yoshitomi not to try to make up any of his own, but use those of the old poets. He must have gotten the one for summer tea ceremony and night viewing confused. Tomomi's face turned dark with fury. And I heard a titter of laughter from the court ladies. I really felt sorry for Yoshitomi.

The tea ceremony did not improve. Indeed, as they say, it went down the mountain from there. For just before the end, Lady Tomaki fainted!

Satsuki May 17, 1858

Lady Tomaki is with child! The Emperor is ecstatic. My mother is happy. So is Auntie, and I for one think it would be very good for Sachi to not be the only Imperial baby. But the rest of the court seems almost evenly divided. Everyone who is happy hopes for a boy. Everyone who is not, hopes for a miscarriage. Is that not awful? I am beginning to think this court is a terrible place. A place of empty rituals and false smiles, cunning courtiers and venomous noble ladies. Would you believe that I heard that the court lady closest to the Emperor's mother put dog excrement in Lady Tomaki's bedding when she was spending time with the Emperor. Is that not the vilest thing one has ever heard?

Satsuki May 20, 1858

The old shogun is dying, they say. Every day here on the palace grounds you see more and more of the great *daimyos* from the shogunate cabinet *bakufu*. They come up from Ninjo castle, which is the center of the shogunate government. This is indeed a change. We hear little, of course, except that the old shogun is dying and that those loyal to the Emperor are dedicated to resisting the treaty with the Americans. Now today we hear that Ii Naosuke, who is in fact the acting shogun, is arriving. People are excited here within the palace. It is as if, finally, people are treating us less as Gods in heaven and more as Japanese people who might have a true connection with our country. For one minute I think of this and I am happy and then the next I am not, because I realize what it means. It means that all this is coming about because for the first time in hundreds and hundreds of years there is to be a bond between the shogunate and the Imperial household and that bond is to be made through Yoshitomi and me.

Later

Ii Naosuke has arrived bearing many presents. Presents from the Americans. These presents were originally taken by the shogun — even those that were expressly for the Emperor. Many courtiers complained. Well, now they are here. Wagons have come through the gates of the palace laden with all sorts of odd things. Many of these gifts were given many years ago when Commodore Perry with his dragon ships first sailed into Shimoda in 1853. And some are new gifts from the new consul, a man named Harris, who stays in the temple in Shimodo. It is he who wants this new treaty signed, which the Emperor rails against.

Satsuki May 22, 1858

The gifts were very tempting. But to my mind, if the Emperor is serious in his rejection of this treaty it seems that he should not accept the gifts. I think he was about to reject them until he saw the miniature steam locomotive. He could not resist! The perfect toy for Sachi and, by this evening, the track was set up near the apartments where Sachi lives with his attendants. We were all required to be present and watch. Lady Tomaki was given the seat of third-highest honor! First-highest honor is the Emperor, the next place is reserved for his mother. His wife, Kujo, looked very sad but the Empress Mother looked like a snake about to strike. The red gash of her mouth parted as I came up to make my obeisance and her blackened teeth showed through her snarl. Lady Tomaki was trembling on her cushioned stool. The tension was so thick, one could cut it with a knife, but suddenly there was a silly *toot-toot* sound, then a puff of steam. The little toy locomotive had commenced its journey, and Sachi, sitting on Iwakura To-momi's lap, drove in the train.

Everyone laughed. The Emperor was completely delighted. Ii Naosuke was whooping. Serving people came with cups of *sake*, rice wine, and people were drinking heavily.

"Stupid!" Auntie hissed.

Pretty soon, all of the courtiers and noble ladies and noblemen and all the *daimyos* who attach themselves to the office of the shogun were quite drunk. The Emperor's previous favorite *nyogo*, Nakayama Yoshiko, who is little Sachi's mother, was giggling lewdly over some joke and pointing at Lady Tomaki. I do not think they noticed me. No one did for that matter, for I had retreated into the shadow of a maple tree, as the day had grown so hot. But I suddenly heard a snakelike hiss. It was none other than the Empress Mother. "You foolish women. You get drunk like this and none of our plans will work. Putting dog excrement in someone's bed is easy. And does nothing. We want to put something else there."

Suddenly, I was very alert. This was obviously about Lady Tomaki, but what could it be? What were they plotting?

Satsuki May 23, 1858

All the noble ladies stink — truly! Some of the gifts from the Americans were bottles of perfumes. They are the worst fragrances I have ever smelled — sharp and bitter. Nothing like incense and sandalwood and our lovely scents. I do not understand what is happening here. The Emperor does not want to make a treaty, but he accepts these gifts — the train, the perfumes. The motto of the *Sonno Joi* movement that supports my brother is "Revere the Emperor. Expel the Barbarians." But I believe now it might be more accurate to say "Revere the Emperor and Smell Like the Barbarians." My brother has always spoken of how — for more than two hundred years — Japan has closed its doors to all foreigners and because of this we have preserved our way. *Sakoku*, my brother believes, is the only way. The very word *sakoku* means "chained." Our country is chained and in this, he believes, lies our salvation. I am not sure what I believe, except perhaps that we are exchanging one set of chains for another.

Satsuki May 24, 1858

I was walking in the garden of the ponds. I had brought my inkstone and folder, as I felt that perhaps I would try to paint the irises that stand knee-deep in the cool water. It was a terribly hot day, and I wore my lightest *yukata*. I felt that making pictures of the irises might make me feel cooler. But my mind was consumed with other thoughts. Precisely, the conversation I overheard between Empress Mother and the court ladies. It frightened me. I was wondering if I should tell Auntie or perhaps go directly to Lady Tomaki, when Yoshitomi stepped out from a small grove of bamboo. I nearly yelped.

"I did not mean to frighten you, Princess," he said.

"I'm not frightened, just surprised."

"I felt the need to talk to you."

This perplexed me and I wondered why, but before I could ask he began to speak, and not in his usual awkward way. His very calmness suddenly engaged me. I felt that he was speaking his own words now and not words that have been put in his mouth by others. "I know you do not like me." I began to protest but he raised a hand to stop my words. "No, it is all right. Perhaps 'do not like' is too strong a way to put it. I know that I would not be your first choice as a husband, or" — his voice dropped very low — "or a lover."

Lover, he said. I was stunned. We are both young, and what do we know about such things? We are only to know about betrothals and marriages. I blinked and looked at him more carefully. He is taller than I thought, and he is not entirely ugly.

"Anyhow," he continued, "I admire and respect you and I know you are very intelligent. Everyone talks of the wonderful poetry you write. I just felt that you should know that I understand this. I understand that I am not your first choice, but I felt that even so, we could still be friends — maybe even good friends. I know that you were betrothed to another who has really captured your heart — Prince Arisugawa. And I, too, have another who has captured my heart."

I am not sure whether I spoke or not. My mouth merely dropped open. I was stunned. And I must admit that I have never felt such a confusing array of emotions. In the first sliver of a second I think I felt insulted. How could anyone else capture his heart? It looks as though he was promised to me now. And then I thought, *how ridiculous of me*, and I nearly laughed out loud, and then I thought, *how wonderful!* How wonderful it is that he is so completely honest. It is so rare, so rare in this court full of deceit and treachery. Although the heat was unbearable that day, it felt as if a cool breeze had suddenly blown through.

I smiled at Yoshitomi. "We most certainly can be friends, Tokugawa Yoshitomi." And I bowed to him, so deeply that my hair brushed the moss. *Either I am getting shorter or my hair is growing longer*, I thought.

Satsuki May 25, 1858
The Time of the Fireflies

I received a gift this morning. It is an exquisite firefly box made from woven bamboo leaves. There is a note with it, written on a sheet of mulberry bark paper.

> *I cannot weave words for a* waka, *but I can make a box for the fireflies that come out tonight for the first time.*
> *Your friend,*
> *Yoshi*

It is the custom for young people to go out on this night and catch fireflies. I shall and hopefully so shall Yoshi. This is the kind of thing that friends do.

Later

I caught fifteen fireflies. They glow now in the corner near my doll altar. They light up the small dolls and make them seem almost ready to step off the altar. I shall release them in the morning. I put a few drops of water in the box for them to drink. I must confess that I was slightly disappointed that Yoshi was not out. He is often required to go to gatherings of the *bakufu* and all the shogun's officers. In fact, most of the time he lives at the Nijo, the shogun's palace. He is, after all, to be the next shogun.

Minazuki June 1, 1858
The Time That the Barley Ripens

The heat grows unbearable. It is not long until we move to the summer Imperial villa, Katsura, on the banks of the Katsura River on the southwest side of the city. The gardens are most beautiful there. There are deep shady glades with pools and stepping-stones across brooks. The breeze blows off the river. Only part of the court goes, as it is not as large as the palace here.

Minazuki June 3, 1858

The June rains have begun. But it is still hot. Auntie and I go to the kennin-ji temple. We need not go in disguise because Auntie goes at this time every year to honor her ancestors on the first day of the rainy season. So this will be the first time I can wear a nice kimono, as I shall not arouse the suspicions of the palace spies. Arisugawa will be there. I shall wear my summer kimono with the waterfall cascading from a mountain cleft and two kingfisher birds soaring. It makes me feel cool just to look at it. It is of hues of blues and misty greens that are perfect for this time of year. I hope Arisugawa thinks I am pretty. It has been several weeks since we have seen each other.

Later

This was our best time yet. Arisugawa and I were left alone to talk in the tea garden between the parts of the ceremony. He got to go to a sumo *beya*, which is like a school or training ground for the wrestlers. He actually met Mashimoto and got to share *chanko nabe* with him! *Chanko nabe* is the hearty stew that all sumo wrestlers eat. He said I would not believe how much they can eat — four bowls for every one of his! He said that Mashimoto was very refined and that he recited some very old Chinese poetry and that it was odd hearing this elegant poetic language coming out of such a huge body. We mostly talked about sumo, but he did notice my kimono, for I received this poem by one of our secret messengers just minutes ago:

> *The kingfisher's gaudy colors*
> *Fade in the mist of true beauty*

Now I am confused. Does he not like my kimono or is this in praise of me? Or maybe he just doesn't like kingfishers? Well, Auntie always says that the best poems have a puzzle at their heart and many layers of meaning. Must stop. Keiko comes with another message. Surely not Arisugawa again so soon.

Minazuki June 4, 1858
The Time That the Mantids Hatch Out

An astonishing piece of . . . of . . . of I am not sure what to call it — news? Or gossip? The message that came late last night was from Yoshi, whom I have not seen since he gave me the bamboo-leaf box for fireflies. It read:

> *Bring the bamboo box and pretend that you are going to catch fireflies. Meet me at the Inari shrine in the garden of the ponds.*

Luckily, it was a moonless night, and I was able to sneak out. I put on my split-toed socks and carried my wooden shoes by their thongs until I got outside to the grass. I started to put them on but then decided I could move faster if I went in my socked feet. So I ran to the garden of the ponds. Inari is the most popular Shinto god, I think, in Japan. There are more shrines to his spirit than any other. It is said that his *kami* can slip into nearly anything from a teapot to a tree. His holy presence is perceived by those few people with second sight. Here, a gnarled and twisted *kuramatsu* tree, a black pine, is said to harbor Inari. A vermilion *torii* gate marks the entrance to the sacred ground of the shrine, and just as I walked through I heard *pssst* from the shrubs along the path. Yoshi stepped out. His face was very tense. He looked so pale, as if he might have seen the *kami* face-to-face.

"What is it?" I asked.

"You know Sano Hidaki?"

"The samurai, the big samurai friend of the chamberlain Tomomi?"

"Yes, that one."

"What about him?"

"He lies now in the sleeping chamber of Lady Tomaki."

"What!" I am appalled.

"It is not what you think."

But my mouth dropped open and no words came out, for I knew not what to think.

Yoshi continued. "He has been put there drunk, and Lady Tomaki is drugged. It is all part of a plot by Iwakui Tomomi and the Empress Mother and others who want to discredit Lady Tomaki in the eyes of the Emperor. I also think that my godfather Ii Naosuke might be a part of all this, for I believe he has yet another *nyogo* picked out for the Emperor. You see, Chikako, it is all part of a plan. They do not revere the Emperor at all. They want only to control him and make him entirely dependent on the shogun, and you and I are part of that plan. There is something in it for everyone. The Empress Mother gets rid of Lady Tomaki, the Emperor's previous favorite *nyogo* will be assured that her son, Sachi, will someday be Emperor."

"And what is there for us, Tokugawa Yoshitomi?" I asked.

"We get nothing. We are pawns in their game and that is why we can risk all to save a good lady."

"And then?"

"And then, well, perhaps we shall get something."

"What?"

"Honor."

In that moment I felt a flicker of what perhaps was love for Yoshi.

"But what are we to do?" I asked, blushing suddenly.

"We have to get him out of there."

"Yoshi, with all respect" — my eyes widened — "do you realize how huge that man is?"

"I know. He is like a sumo wrestler. But you have a maid, right?"

"Keiko." Then the idea sprang to life. "Yes, Keiko has a very large brother. He works in the guardhouse and stables."

"And I saw him moving the new Buddha statue the other day to the pavilion in the Court of Cool Breezes. That was huge."

"Let me go find Keiko."

"Go fast."

I found Keiko and explained the problem. She quickly ran for her brother. We met at the torii gate of the Inari shrine. They were there fast. Suddenly, Matsui did not seem as large as before. I felt as if goldfish were swimming in my stomach. I was not sure if he could do this. Then Yoshi announced, "We must all help."

And so we did. I held my breath while we walked, for fear of hitting with my foot a nightingale board. These are made from the wood of the cypress and tweet like nightingales when walked upon. But they are mostly in the apartments of the Emperor. It is a kind of protection to warn him and his guards if someone approaches who is unannounced. Before we even entered the sleeping chamber, we could hear the loud snores of Sano Hidaki, and they were enough to cover any tweets of the nightingale boards. It was apparent that even Lady Tomaki's maid, who slept outside the chamber on a futon, had been drugged. When we entered, all we could see was this immense hulk of a man. His snores were so loud that the paper in the *shoji* screens trembled. I could not even see Lady Tomaki until we were right next to the futon. She was curled in his shadow and lay so still that I thought she was dead. Matsui directed us. Keiko and I were to take his feet and Yoshi and Matsui would lift him from the shoulders. On the count of three we began. I closed my eyes and concentrated. I was the smallest of the four of us and the weakest, but I willed myself to do this. Yoshi's word hummed in my brain. *We get nothing. We are pawns in their game and that is why we can risk all to save a good lady. . . . Well, perhaps we shall get something. . . . Honor.*

I have never felt such a weight in my life. My muscles, muscles I did not know existed in my stomach and arms, clinched. I shut my eyes and bit down on my lip. *I must do this. I must do this. I will do this.*

"We do not have to go far," Yoshi kept saying. "Just to the torii gate. It will look like he was seeking blessings from Inari." We set him down twice to rest on our way to the torii gate. Each time I had to make my arms and hands and mind like iron to pick him up again. Sano Hidaki never even flickered an eyelid. His snores continued to saw the night air in the same rhythm. Finally, we got to the gate and set him down. We were completely exhausted.

Before we said good night, Yoshi said suddenly, "Chikako, why is your chin dripping with blood?"

I touched my chin. My fingers came away bloody. I had bitten through my lip!

"Bushido," Yoshi whispered softly and smiled.

An hour has now passed and I cannot believe that he used this word with me — *bushido* — it means the way of the samurai. It is the most important belief of the samurai warriors, which holds that ordinary people are free to seek pleasure or personal gain, but only warriors, samurai, pursue the higher values, glory in hardship, and are ready to accept pain, and even death, for principles of honor. Was there ever a girl warrior, a woman samurai? I might be the first to have ever heard this word used to describe something a girl had done. And the girl is me! I keep licking my cut lip and hope that the sting will stay for a bit.

Minazuki June 6, 1858

Our plan worked. One could see the sour looks on the Empress Mother's and Iwakura Tomomi's faces. But Yoshi says we must be alert. They will plan something else.

I wonder sometimes who this girl is who captured Yoshi's heart. I would like to know about her but am afraid to ask, or perhaps I am afraid to hear about her.

My lip looks bruised. Mother and Auntie asked me what happened, and I told them that I accidentally bit down on it. They seemed to accept this. It has been tender but now it grows less so every hour of the day. I shall rather miss this sign of my *bushido*.

Minazuki June 12, 1858

The shogun has died. The word came this morning from Edo. I wonder when Yoshi will become the new shogun. Yoshi has been whisked away. We did not even get to say good-bye. Ii Naosuke took him off. No one is quite sure to where, either Edo, or others say to the port city of Yokohama.

Minazuki June 15, 1858

There is talk of many disturbances in the wake of the old shogun's death. Some resent Ii Naosuke's power. There were a few *daimyo* who wanted another young man to be the new shogun. His name is Hitotsubashi Yoshinobu, and he comes from another clan than the Tokugawa shoguns. It is all very confusing, but there are rumors of great unrest and even violence. In light of this, I do believe that the little drama with Lady Tomaki has been forgotten — at least temporarily.

It seems to me that there is a tension that hangs over everything. Auntie barely gets her nose out of her astrologer's almanac. The days are long and hot and rainy.

People's tempers are short. Auntie snapped at me when I asked if we might have an outing with Arisugawa to another sumo tournament. "You touch a turtle and thank the *kami* you saw him when you did!" She scowled and went back to her almanac. I felt my insides turn dark. *Touch a turtle!* Indeed. That is Auntie's personal good-luck animal. I am both angered and confused. Why should I need luck now? It was Auntie who started the whole business of my seeing Arisugawa. It is as if she is blaming me.

Later

Would I rather have Auntie mad or my mother sad? I met my mother in the hall of golden peacocks unexpectedly today, and she gasped when she saw me and her eyes brimmed with tears. She ran off without saying anything!

This is all very strange.

Minazuki June 16, 1858
The Time of the Second Rice Sprouting

Before I went to bed last night, I found beside my futon an *omokage* rose blossom floating in a porcelain bowl with a lovely design. It was a bowl I had never seen, but one could tell by the design it was quite old. There was a poem beside it, written on the special mulberry bark paper that only Auntie uses.

Wintry looks
Belie one who
Shall guard spring's chance

This poem is very mysterious. It is an apology I am sure, but there is a much deeper meaning. I feel a threat, not from Auntie, never. Perhaps she warns me of some danger. But why can't she speak? I feel very alone. I wish Yoshi was here at the palace. And I wish I could visit with Arisugawa. Even Keiko seems suddenly distant, and she and I giggled and were very close right after our nighttime adventure of heaving Sano Hidaki out of Lady Tomaki's sleeping chamber. There was new intimacy that I have never had with a servant and which I think we both knew was wrong, but still rather enjoyable.

Minazuki June 18, 1858

For two nights I have had a very disturbing dream. But when Auntie has asked about my dreams these last two days, I have lied. I have dreamed of the moon falling. This is a very bad sign. It means illness hovers and that someone will soon become sick.

Minazuki June 19, 1858

Well, no one has fallen ill, but I sit here stunned. The Empress Mother's first lady-in-waiting has come to tell me and Auntie and my mother that the date has been set for my teeth-blackening ceremony. It is to be in November at the time of the chrysanthemum festival. Lady Tomaki was here taking tea with us, and she gasped and reached for my hand. The lady-in-waiting gave her a narrow, mean look so like that of her mistress. There seemed to be a warning in the look and surely as soon as the lady-in-waiting left, my mother turned to Lady Tomaki and said, "Don't, Tomaki-san — don't interfere. I know you would go to the Emperor. But it is too great a risk."

Auntie bowed her head and looked into her teacup and mumbled something.

So what does this mean?

First of all, it means an insult to my mother.

Second, it means that it has been decided that I shall soon be married, for teeth-blackening usually precedes the ceremony by a year or so. And third, it means that the engagement to Arisugawa will definitely be broken. I feel my heart crumble.

Minazuki June 19, 1858

Now there are rumors that my birthday is to be changed and even worse, I am to be adopted. Oh, my mother and Auntie will still take care of me, but often children, especially boys, are given the name of an adopted family for political reasons. Or if a *daimyo*, for instance, hasn't a male heir, he might adopt one from another family, allowing both families to carry on its traditions. I know exactly what will happen to me. I will be adopted by Kujo the Empress's family, thus giving the Imperial family an even stronger and more valid connection to the new shogun — for remember, my mother was not a wife but a *nyogo*. This plan has the marks, however, of the Empress Mother, not the Empress, all over it. So they will take away my birthday and then they will erase my real mother. In every book of Imperial lineage, her name will be crossed out and the Empress Kujo's written in. And I will be required to make my bows and kowtows to her with all the names and titles that one uses for one's parents.

Later

I have received a gift from my brother the Emperor: a black lacquer box inlaid with the design of a golden chrysanthemum. Like an ornate bribe, it sits on my table. The chrysanthemum, of course, is a subtle reminder of my teeth-blackening ceremony that will come in the season for chrysanthemums.

Minazuki June 20, 1858

Tomorrow is the summer solstice and my mother and Auntie and I shall go to the Kamigamo shrine for the purification ceremony. We are, of course, to attend first a solstice ceremony here, but Auntie scowls that it will count for nothing because nothing can be purified in the filthy atmosphere that seeps through this court. I have never seen Auntie so grim.

Today the rains falls softly and the colors of the hydrangeas are the most beautiful when it rains. I am tempted to get out my inkstone and brushes and recall the Four Gentlemen to help me capture their beauty. Yes, perhaps this will calm me, for these do not seem like happy times to me, with my nightmares of falling moons and my daydreams of black teeth.

Minazuki June 21, 1858

I think I really am in love! Arisugawa was at the Kamigamo shrine. I had not expected him, especially since my mother was to accompany Auntie and me, but he was there and the whole time was perfect. Not just because of him, but because it was such a relief from the palace. I think I have discovered what has drawn me to Arisugawa all these years. I write here now my most private thoughts to recount how this feeling stole upon me. For a time, I think I might have had doubts. For I was attracted to Yoshi recently, but I sense the difference now between two kinds of love. What I feel for Yoshi is the coziness of friendship. He shall always be my friend, but what I feel for Arisugawa is a blending of spirits and souls that feels as if we have shared a bond in previous lifetimes and will continue to share it in the thousands of years and possibly lifetimes to come. It is this bond that defines our very essence. This realization came to me in the middle of the purification ceremony. And this ceremony was as Auntie said, an "antidote" to the one held in the palace that afternoon.

It was a long trip to the shrine. Keiko and my mother's maid Atsuko accompanied us with *bento* boxes filled with my favorite foods — *mochi*, rice cakes, special pickles, and *minazuki* cakes. These cakes are the seasonal sweet made by spreading red bean paste on top of sweet rice jelly. They are said to ward off evil and protect one from summer heat. We ate a few of these on our way in the palanquin. As we passed through the red torii gates leading into the shrine, Auntie recited an ancient poem composed just for this shrine.

The wind stirring, Nara Brook at dusk —
The purification rite is the sign of summer

Right then, I felt the first invisible specks of the dirt begin to dissolve from my mind. The Shinto priests dressed in their white vestments had already assembled in the courtyard of the *hosodono*, the main meditation hall, as we climbed out of our palanquin in front of the pavilion with two sacred sand cones. On the ground, the silver ring of maiden grass had been lit, and the priests passed through this ring twice, once to the right and once to the left. Then we were to follow. Arisugawa fell in beside me and, as we both stepped across this ring of fire and lifted our clothing, we looked into each other's eyes. Our heads were bent down slightly to be mindful of the fire, and I could see the flames reflected in his, and he must have seen them in my eyes as well. He smiled and my heart stirred. Was it a feeling of love or absolute purity that had begun to steal over me, or perhaps both? The aura of his karma seemed to glimmer and perhaps mine did as well. And I felt for the first time the true meaning of karma: that both of us had a fate, a destiny that was part of a very timeless cycle.

At the Kamigamo shrine there are two brooks that have converged right at the main temple and then veer off in separate directions into the woods. One brook is broad and slow, the other narrow and fast. Auntie calls them the "he brook" and the "she brook," in just the same way, I suppose, that in many of our gardens the larger more forceful waterfall is called the "he waterfall" while the gentler one is called the "she waterfall."

We walked to just the point where the two brooks meet. There is a fountain to mark the place, and there were two very ancient priests. From their baskets we took the cutout paper figures of a man and a woman. On these figures, we wrote our names and our ages and our birthdays. I actually wrote down my real birthday — August 1 in the year of the Fire Horse — and then we walked across a little stone bridge and followed the "he brook" by walking beside a lovely forest. When we were far into the forest, we took our paper cutouts and sent them fluttering down the stream. Behind us in the distance we heard priests chanting the purification prayers. Auntie and Mother stood a bit away from us and watched. Then Arisugawa and I took our *bento* boxes from Keiko and found a place on a rock close by the stream and ate our rice cakes and pickles and *minazuki* pastries.

We talked of many things. I told him about the teeth-blackening ceremony and the changing of my birthday and yes, the threat to our engagement. He says they can, with their words, change my birthday, but it is meaningless. Then he said the best thing. "You and I, Chikako, were both born in the years that have signs of incredible faithfulness and strength. So we are known for our steadfastness in all things. With such strong signs as we both have, our two destinies according to the laws of the cosmos cannot be changed no matter what."

I then told him what Yoshi and I had done that night with Keiko and her brother's help. I had wondered if I should tell him what Yoshi said about the *bushido*, and that I possessed the way of the warrior. I was not sure if he would understand. But I finally told him, and he grew very still. For several moments I was nervous. And then he looked at me and said, "Tokugawa Yoshitomi must not only be very smart but have a very deep heart. For it takes such a heart and a mind to know you I think, Chikako. He honors you. Such a friend is precious."

Later

A messenger came on this the shortest night of the year. The messenger arrived with a *waka* for me.

> *May I honor the warrior woman*
> *The way snow on a branch in April*
> *Honors the pink of the cherry blossoms*
> *I stand in awe of fragile miracles*

I shall treasure this poem forever. It seals our karma, I do believe.

So I write a poem which I have been thinking about since I saw Arisugawa on this day.

Are we not like two birds
Flying with one wing
Through many lifetimes?

Later

I cannot sleep. Perhaps I worry about dreaming of falling moons. The fireflies are thick outside. I can see their light like pale splotches on my paper window. I get my bamboo cage, the one that Yoshi gave me. How much more I treasure that simple woven cage than the black-and-gold box my brother gave me. I go out to catch the fireflies.

Minazuki June 23, 1858
The Time That the Deer Break Antlers

Everyone is in a flurry today as we pack to go to the summer Imperial villa, Katsura.

When will I see Arisugawa again? When will I see my good friend Yoshi again? Yoshi is in Edo, I guess, learning how to be shogun. Although it is said he has been preparing for this since he was very young.

Auntie does not seem quite right to me. Her color is odd, especially the white part of her eyes. They look like tea.

Minazuki June 28, 1858
Katsura Imperial Villa, Kyoto

We arrived here at Katsura four days ago. The move took a lot out of Auntie. She is still exhausted and lies abed most of the day. I can tell that Mother is worried, too, but she says that Auntie will get better, that Katsura is a healing place because it is so quiet. Only a fraction of the court can come here as there are not enough accommodations for everyone. This is very good. Many of the court ladies, especially the *tsubone*, the lower-ranked ones, have been left behind. It seems that it is the *tsubone* who give us the most trouble. They happen to be the same ones who despise Lady Tomaki. I think the Emperor is fed up with all this bickering over his favorite *nyogo* now. He has too many other things on his mind. Rumor has it that he is not pleased, for some reason, with Ii Naosuke. I am not sure why. But perhaps I shall not have to marry Yoshi. He can just remain my good friend. In a perfect world, Arisugawa would be my husband and Yoshi my dear friend. I do often wonder what the girl is like who captured Yoshi's heart. I wonder if I dare ever ask him?

I do like our apartments here at Katsura. There are three main parts to the villa: the *ko-shoin*, the old; *chu-shoin*, the middle; and the *shin-shoin*, the new hall. But we are in none of those, I am pleased to report. No. Rather, the Emperor has assigned us to a newly built, smaller building. We think he built this especially for Lady Tomaki so that he might remove her from prying eyes and the vicious court ladies — including the Empress Mother. But he has arranged within this building apartments for Mother, Auntie, and me. There is only space, however, for two servants: my maid, Keiko, and Atsuko, mother's maid. But this is fine. The best part is that we are close to the *gepparo* teahouse. There are, in all, four teahouses — one for each season. The *gepparo*, or the moon-crescent teahouse, also has a pavilion for moon viewing in the fall. So now it is quiet in the summer. It is the perfect place for Auntie's health to be restored.

Fumizuki July 1, 1858
The Time When Cicadas Begin to Sing

Indeed, the cicadas' singing is so loud on these nights that I often find it hard to sleep at first, but now they are perhaps a distraction from Auntie's breathing. She suffers a chest congestion. A doctor has been summoned, a royal physician. I think this might not have happened had the Emperor not been here visiting Lady Tomaki and seen Auntie for himself. He is quite fond of Auntie. And he does seem troubled these days. But he says he enjoys his visits to our little pavilion. We have already once taken tea together in the *gepparo*, which is never used this time of year, but it was so close two servants carried Auntie there. And there was a moon just rising, a sliver of one, and we watched its reflection dance on the water like a silver minnow. For a while, Auntie seemed to grow better but now she is worse. We wait for the doctor. In the meantime, my mother, who is an expert blender of incense, has made up a mixture that is said to date back to the time of Prince Toshito, who built Katsura many hundreds of years before. He, too, was known as a master blender of incense. In a mortar, she combined cloves and pulverized seashells and many lotus leaves, for lotus leaves are the main ingredients for the summer incense fragrance. Keiko helped, as all of these ingredients must be pounded three thousand times to make the fine dust that we hope will drive out the spirits when burned.

In the middle of all this, Lady Tomaki arrived, very agitated. She says not only is the physician coming but a famous *genza*, an exorcist. The Emperor feels that an angry spirit has settled within Auntie. The *genza*, whose name is Nariako, is to arrive momentarily. The apartments must be prepared. Three more servants seemed to melt out of thin air. The paper-screen windows were slid open so that the spirits may leave. And then a girl slipped into the corner of the room. My heart lurched. Now I know how sick Auntie must be. This girl, who is about my age, is the spirit catcher. She has no name or if she does we shall never know it. She is an *eta*, an outcast. This means that she belongs to the lowest rank of society. Her father might be a butcher or perhaps an executioner or a tanner. They are considered polluted, but their children often work as spirit catchers. When the *genza* flings the bad spirit out of Auntie this girl will catch it. Until this moment Auntie's illness had not been real to me. Now it is.

Later

The *genza* Nariako was nearly as old and small as Auntie. He arrived with two assistants. They handed the spirit catcher a hollow gourd. And then they began to chant the mantra of the transformed heart. It is an old incantation that has been used for everything from leprosy to difficult childbirth. We were all given fans to help waft the spirit when it was drawn out toward the girl who sat with her gourd. A snarl crawled across her face and soon her features were as grotesque as those of a devil mask in a Noh play. Her eyes rolled back in her head. She began to shriek. Of course, the shrieks were not hers but the spirit that was being pulled from Auntie's body and beginning to enter hers. So she cupped the gourd to her breast. This was a sign that the spirit was entirely within her.

The *genza* now began shouting in a voice that surprised me for its strength coming out of such a shriveled body. "Identify yourself, spirit. Name thy name." But the no-name girl seemed to gag and collapsed back on the cushions. The *genza* nodded at one of our servants to prop her up, and I could tell that they did not want to touch her, but they did. The *genza* demanded again that the spirit identify itself and state its grievance. The spirit could have been anything — the ghost of a dead person who was still attempting to cling to life because of some unhappiness not resolved by death, or it could have been the spirit from a living person who is filled still with poisonous thoughts and jealousies. This was what I feared. But still nothing came forth from the no-name girl. Auntie, however, seemed better — her breathing more even, her color less sallow. Finally, the *genza* gave up. The *eta* collapsed senseless and was removed from the apartments.

Later

I cannot believe it. Auntie is sitting up and taking small little tastes of *yama* snow. *Yama* snow is one of our favorite summer dishes. Snow and ice from the mountain is stored in the icehouse. We sent Keiko to bring back a bucket of it and then it was mounded into silver bowls and drizzled with vine syrup. It is very good and refreshing. Mother and I take turns spooning the ice into Auntie's mouth, and it takes so long it is almost melted, but still the sugar will give her strength. If only Auntie can keep getting better. It worries me, however, that the *genza* could not force the spirit to identify itself. I think it makes all of us nervous. An evil unnamed is almost more frightening than one that is named. Perhaps I am thinking this evil has no name. Perhaps it is like the *eta* girl.

Fumizuki July 2, 1858

I have not practiced my *koto* for a long time, but here at Katsura I do, indeed, love practicing by a pavilion near the pond. My teacher, Sensei Ayakana Mimiko, came this morning and Keiko and Atsuko set up my *koto* and my sensei's side by side on the pavilion. We were close enough so that Auntie could hear our music. When Ayakana Mimiko plays, it is beautiful but when I pluck the thirteen strings sometimes it sounds as if a half dozen warblers are being strangled. In playing the *koto* one must pluck certain strings while pressing and pulling others. Each string has a name, and I seem to have trouble with the number five and number six string. Poor Auntie, if she heard this! But I beseeched my honorable teacher to play the entire song through at the end of our lesson so that Auntie might have something fine to fill her ears at last.

Fumizuki July 3, 1858

We have just received terrible news. Two days ago a foreign ship, an American ship, entered Yokohama harbor. The Emperor is furious. He is furious with the shogunate for allowing this to happen. He is furious with the *daimyo*, for he thinks they have betrayed him. I do not understand why this is happening now. I thought the shogunate was devoted to the Emperor. Whatever happened to those who shouted, "Revere the Emperor. Expel the Barbarians."?

What is to happen to my marriage to Yoshi? I have many mixed feelings about this. Arisugawa is my true love, but I certainly do not want Yoshi to be my brother's enemy. It was not, of course, Yoshi who caused this to happen with the ship in Yokohama. It was Ii Naosuke. Yoshi is merely his puppet, and that man frightens me. I think that is perhaps the worse part of everything. Yoshi is nothing but a puppet, and if we do marry he shall be a puppet husband and I shall be his puppet wife in a puppet marriage where Ii Naosuke will pull the strings. That is no life. I would prefer, I think, being a Buddhist nun in a convent where one can take refuge in dharma, the teachings of Buddha, and truly learn how to care for people and seek blessings for all living things.

Later

I have thought more about becoming a nun. I think I might like that very much. But then I think of these other things that one might become that are all so opposite of being a puppet in a puppet life. There are many things I would like to do that I feel are real things and that, in one way or another, permit one to follow the teachings of Buddha and take refuge not just in dharma, but in *sangha*, as well, which is one's commitment to the community and not just individuals.

When I first thought of some of the things one could

be, it surprised me, for I realized that they were fun as well as serving in the pathway of Buddha. Here is a list:

1) A confectioner of tea sweets for tea ceremonies.
2) A moss gardener or a leaf arranger, like the ones I see out my window picking some twigs from the velvety moss so that it may look perfect, or arranging a pattern of bright-colored leaves on the surface of a pond so that people might contemplate their beauty against the black, silky water.
3) A superb musician like Sensei Ayakana.
4) A poet.

Fumizuki July 6, 1858
The Time of the Hot Winds

Tomorrow is the *Tanabata* festival. Today Mother and I and Lady Tomaki shall go to the Kennin-ji temple to offer prayers for Auntie's recovery. All the signs for traveling to that temple on this day are very favorable according to the calendar. How long ago it seems now that Auntie and I first went there on such an unlucky day, in disguise so I might meet with Arisugawa. I miss him so. I wonder if there might be any chance of his being there today. What a selfish girl I am. I must think of Auntie, not my own desires — and yet I do. For, after all, *Tanabata* is called the Star Festival. It celebrates the old Chinese legend of the two stars that were lovers, the Cowherd Star and the Weaver Star that are separated and are allowed just once a year to meet on the starry bridge that crosses the river of heaven, the Milky Way. Such a romantic story. And some say this is the day and the night when many such lovers who are, for one reason or another separated, meet again. I shall indeed, however, write my wish on a strip of paper and attach it to a branch of bamboo at the temple, as is the custom. But my wish and my prayers shall be for Auntie's recovery.

Fumizuki July 7, 1858

It is very late. It took the bearers of our palanquin forever to thread their way through the streets crowded with festival goers. While we were bogged down in the traffic I saw something unbelievable. Even now as I write these words I cannot believe what my eyes saw. But they did see it. And he saw me, and he knew that I saw him and who he was with. It was Yoshi in the disguise of a street cleaner dressed in the shaggy, straw rain cape of a peasant and a broad straw hat. In one hand, he held the pointed stick with which he stabbed the litter to pick it up and in his other, he held the hand of a young girl.

The young girl was an *eta*, and not just any *eta* but, indeed, the spirit catcher who had come to catch the demon that the *genza* had driven out when he came to cure Auntie. My mouth went dry. Our palanquin had stopped dead, and I had drawn back the curtain just a bit. Thankfully, I was alone, for Lady Tomaki and my mother rode together in another palanquin. My eyes were fixed on Yoshi. He did not see me at first, for he was looking down and speaking and giggling with the girl — this no-name girl whose father is perhaps a butcher of animals or an executioner of men or a cleaner of public toilets. And there was my dear friend Yoshi actually holding her hand! *So this is the girl who has captured his heart,* I thought, and just at that moment his eyes raised and stared straight into mine. It was as if the world went silent for the two of us. A look of utter shock crossed his face, turning it pale. The noise of the street seemed to vanish. From the corner of my eye, right next to my palanquin I saw a large bowl crash to the ground and shatter from a pottery stall, but I heard nothing. I did not breathe. I was in a state of some kind of numbness. And then my palanquin lurched ahead.

So that is what I saw. I do not know what to think. Yoshi has brought on nothing but trouble for himself. An *eta*! Why an *eta*? A merchant's daughter, a farmer's daughter, anyone but an *eta*. It is utterly unthinkable. Yet he has allowed this to happen.

Fumizuki July 9, 1858
The Time When Crickets Come into Walls

A note from Yoshi has arrived. Indeed, his best poem yet — such does love inspire.

> *There is no reason for the heart's path*
> *No more so than*
> *For the trail of a falling petal caught in a gust*

And all I want to write back is "But an *ETA!* Tell me you are joking, foolish boy!"

Fumizuki July 10, 1858

I am required to attend *ukai*. This is a fishing expedition using cormorants as the fish catchers. It is one of the most ancient and noble sports and a favorite of my brother the Emperor. I really do not want to go, but mother says I must. We will go in the evening just after dark.

Later there were six boats. Lady Tomaki and I rode in the *ubone* with my brother. This is a great honor. I was shocked to see that the Empress Mother had not been invited, but the Emporer's wife, Kujo, sat with my mother. This was interesting. I think my brother is up to something. Perhaps all he is up to is harmony in his time of worry with the shogunate and the American ships. He knows that my mother and Kujo were once close, and he knows that his own mother is nothing but a trouble-maker. Oh well, I try not to think about this.

There was much I try not to think about these days — Yoshi and the *eta*. Becoming a puppet wife.

There was a brazier of coals, which flared with flames, hanging from a pole off the bow of the boat. The reflection of the flames on the water attracted the fish. The reflec-tions attracted me. There was something restful about watching the dance of flames on the water's surface. The *usho*, who is the main bird handler, sat in the bow of the boat with my brother. When the fish began to swarm, the two head cormorants, whose leashes the *usho* and my brother held, dove. If they are good, and these were, they return with the sweet fish called *ayu*. The cormorants wear rings around their necks that prevent them from swallowing the fish.

To some this might seem sad, but these cormorants are well-fed and live twice as long as other cormorants. But they are never free. It is some price to pay, I do believe. It seems more and more to me that there are prices to pay for many things.

Fumizuki July 12, 1858

Auntie has asked that we have a tea ceremony this day. I am not sure why, but she wants one. She insists that she is to be the host.

She has invited Ayakana, my music sensei, to be a guest and requests that between the two acts of the tea ceremony Ayakana and I play the *koto*. So I must go now and practice, for I do want my playing to be very fine. Auntie really asks for so little.

Later

Auntie has died! She died between the second and third cups of tea. Between the thick tea and the thin tea, our dear host departed.

Fumizuki July 13, 1858
Just before dawn

I cannot sleep. I feel, however, a deep peace. I believe that Auntie planned her death. Is it not odd that she hosted this last tea ceremony? I finally begin to understand the meaning of the way of tea, which we call *chanoyu*. There is water and there is fire, opposing forces that are brought into balance, and by carefully following the ritual, a spirit begins to flood throughout one's being. There is a kind of communication and with that comes a relaxation. I think I knew as I drank the second cup of thick tea, as Auntie so perfectly wiped the cups and turned the prettiest part of the design of the plovers in flight toward me, that this was her way of saying good-bye. It was as if she had said, "I am well, you are well. Now let me go." She preferred not to go out onto the pavilion between the two cups, but to wait. She asked Ayakana and me to play "Ode to Autumn." It is a simple composition. When we returned for the third cup of the thin tea, Auntie was lying on her side. Peaceful, her hands, having just wiped the cup, still seemed to hold it but the cup was turned with its plovers in flight toward me.

I shall miss Auntie, but I am not exactly sad. She led a long life with a deep sense of harmony and beauty and she was no one's puppet — no, never — for she was a true spirit. Her life and her death are examples of perfect karma. For the laws of karma say that every action has an effect. Her good life brought a good death and the promise of a future good life. Now the time of mourning begins, but in a sense it shall be a celebration. A celebration of Auntie's karma.

Later

My brother has requested that I be the Caller for Auntie. It is a great honor. But it is one I do not want. I am to go to the roof of the palace, carrying her kimono, then turn in each of the four directions of the earth and call her spirit back from the land of the dead. The spirit only comes back if it has died in a troubled or unpurified state. But this is not Auntie. When the spirit flies back, the Caller folds it into the kimono, which is then placed on top of the funeral pyre. Auntie's kimono, however, shall be empty. She is at peace.

Fumizuki July 14, 1858

I went to be my auntie's Caller. There was a fine drizzle. Scarves of mist floated through the air like spirits, but not my auntie's, and a cloud bit the edge of the moon. So I waved my auntie's kimono and said the chants, then sprinkled rice to scatter any evil spirits and folded up the kimono. I knew it was empty. I knew my auntie was free. Indeed, I quickly had the proof. For so strong was her karma that she pushed away the cloud that bit the moon, and it shined bright even through the drizzling rain.

And now today, I have just returned from the burning grounds where Auntie's body was put upon the pyre. At first, there were huge orange flames that leaped like devils above the pyre. The air turned wavy with the intensity of the heat. I held my wooden prayer beads and whispered the sutra to myself as the Buddhist monks chanted theirs. After a while, when the flames had consumed all that had been Auntie's material being on this earth, I watched the trails of black smoke rise and stretch into snakes against the sky, and finally grow thin and vanish. It was then I knew she was really gone.

We — my mother, my brother the Emperor, and I — were her closest remaining family, so we brought the urn with her ashes back to our apartments where we will keep it in a place of honor for thirty-five days with incense sticks burning about it on a small altar. Then after thirty-five days we shall take it to the Buddhist burial ground.

Fumizuki July 21, 1858
The Time When Rotted Weeds Turn to Fireflies

Keiko came to me this morning with an odd look on her face. She announced that Yoshi was here to pay his respects and deliver his condolences over the death of Auntie. What would I do? Were we to talk about the *eta* girl? Then it struck me that Keiko, too, must know about this girl and she knew that I knew, or why would she have had that strange look on her face? Well, I went to receive him in our most formal room, the twelve-mat tatami room where Auntie's urn is kept. We spoke in the manner that one is to speak when paying such a call of sadness. But all I could think of was the sadness that was unspoken was greater than the sadness of which we spoke. Auntie departed this earth with her karma strong, but Yoshi's karma — well, I dread to think of what his actions might cause in this life and a future life. This, to me, is unbearably sad. When we were coming back from the burning grounds and when I looked out my palanquin window, I saw many of these *eta*. They congregate around the burial plain since they are involved with the tasks of death, building the great pyres, lighting the fires, and raking the coals. They are raggedy and dirty-looking and many speak in a strange tongue that seems to me not quite Japanese. I looked for that *eta* girl, but did not see her. She could have been there very easily, however. And now the boy whose heart she has captured and is to be my husband came to me to tell me of his sadness of my auntie's passing. I wanted to cry out loud to Yoshi, "You are alive! Why must you let the things of death cling to you, as it will if you bind your heart to this *eta* girl?"

Fumizuki July 30, 1858

Something strange is going on here in the summer palace. Many *daimyos* arrived this morning. These lords rarely visit the Emperor at our summer villa. There is no room, for one thing. And now it is reported that the Emperor shall return to the Imperial palace immediately. I do hope we shall not have to return. I want to remain here longer, here in the place where Auntie last breathed.

Fumizuki July 31, 1858

The Emperor has been insulted. By Ii Naosuke. So this was what all the strangeness was about. Ii Naosuke has signed a treaty with the American man named Harris. It is said he did so because this man Harris said that if Japan did not sign the treaty, the same fate that happened to China would happen to our country. But I do not understand what happened to China. I wish someone would explain. Now our port will officially be open for trade with other countries. That is all I know.

Hazuki August 1, 1858

This is my real birthday, the day I was born in the year of the Fire Horse. I commemorate it in my own very private way. My brother is a weak Emperor and what with Auntie gone, I think that I shall need a bit of the Fire Horse in me to get through the manipulations of the Empress Mother and Ii Naosuke.

Hazuki August 2, 1858

News leaks in slowly, drip by drip. It is said that the treaty was signed because foreign invaders from a land called England came and murdered people in China. It might be just a rumor but it was enough to scare Ii Naosuke and the rest of the *bakufu* into making this treaty.

Later

Another rumor — or perhaps it is true. I do not know, but it has been said that some *daimyo* and samurai have been killed by the supporters of Ii Naosuke. I think that all I hear about these days, all I see, is death, death, death. Naosuke is Yoshi's adopted father. Is he a murderer, my future father-in-law? And my husband who holds the hand of an *eta*, is he not doomed?

I desperately want to see Arisugawa. Arisugawa is life!

Hazuki August 3, 1858

All I think about is seeing Arisugawa. I am desperate.

Hazuki August 4, 1858

I have confided my despair to Keiko.

Later

Keiko comes to me. She has thought of a way for me to see Arisugawa secretly. I dare not explain it here until it has happened.

Hazuki August 7, 1858

It has happened. Keiko somehow got a message to an aunt of hers who is a moss gardener at the shrine of the Katsura River, where mother and Auntie and I went so many months ago for the *Nagashi bina* ceremony. Her aunt knows a kindly nun there who is, I believe, very romantic and has a connection with Arisugawa's family. So, indeed, a meeting was planned. A tryst arranged. Yes, Arisugawa and I met by the river once more. I went in disguise. And this perhaps is the strangest thing. Keiko told me that it would still be dangerous to leave the summer villa grounds, even in a palanquin lacking the Imperial crests. We would still be noticed, as these palace grounds are smaller and have fewer people. So it was my idea that she fetch for me a straw rain cape, wide straw hat, straw sandals — just like the peasants wear! I tucked in my hair to look like a boy. In short, I looked just like Yoshi when he went to meet his *eta*, except I go to meet my Prince!

We sat by the river once again and talked. Arisugawa said it is true that Ii Naosuke has had people murdered and then, almost apologetically, he said that although this is terrible, the good part might be that there are voices rising against my marriage to Yoshi. I did not tell Arisugawa about Yoshi and the *eta*. I feel that such terrible things need not be known by all.

Hazuki August 9, 1858
The Time That the White Dew Falls

Yoshi is no longer Yoshi. He is now Tokugawa Iemochi, fourteenth shogun of the Tokugawa shogunate. He was just designated by Ii Naosuke. And now, apparently, all anyone talks about is if I shall be offered up as his bride. Even here at the summer villa I feel all eyes upon me. I care not to leave my apartments. I cannot stand the staring, and it is not as if I have anything to say about it. As if even my mother or the Emperor has anything to say about it. We are truly prisoners of heaven, for the water lilies bloom on all the ponds, and a carpet of violets nod their tiny heads in the shade of a maple outside my paper window. Yes. Jailed in heaven, yet my predicament is little different from that of a common thief.

Hazuki August 15, 1858

Tonight is the night of the *Bon* festival when the souls of the dead are welcomed back. Lady Tomaki came this morning, and with Mother and myself, we selected lanterns to set out to guide Auntie's soul back to us. In our twelve-mat tatami room we shall also set out food. Mother has already been in touch with the pastry chef. We will have all the typical sweets for August — bush clover dew, waterfall wafers and pinks, always a favorite of Auntie's, and green maple leaf. We open the paper window so the first of autumn's cool breezes can blow through from our private gardens. Outside I see the old, black pine that humps low across the ground like a somewhat weary dragon. I hope that Auntie can find her way back to us for this night. We have prepared all for her excellent soul. And tomorrow it will be thirty-five days since Auntie has died, and we shall take the urn with her ashes to the Buddhist cemetery near Kennin-ji temple.

We hear that the Empress Mother is upset that we shall not have the *Tsukimi*, or moon viewing. The Emperor wants to delay this until after Auntie's urn burial. He says it is only proper. The Empress Mother is very angry, as she has invited many of her closest noble ladies, for whom there is not usually room here at the villa, for the moon viewing. I hope she does not cause trouble. She is a woman of small spirit and might think of ways to do mischief, to try and show her power. The Empress Mother does not like being told no by anyone, even her own son, the Emperor.

Hazuki August 17, 1858
The Time for the Rice to Ripen

We took Auntie's urn to the cemetery. As the priests were chanting the burial prayers, I seemed to feel a presence. A wind stirred in the black pines at the edge of the cemetery, and my attention was drawn to this small grove of trees that seemed to mirror the bent shapes of the priests. A shadow caught my eye. It was Arisugawa, of this I am sure. He had come to bid my auntie a final farewell. We could not, of course, meet because the Emperor and his mother were both there. But even though we could not meet, our spirits seemed to flow together. I could not help but think of the *Tanabata* festival that celebrates the once-yearly meeting of the Cowherd Star and the Weaver Star on the starry bridge of the Milky Way. I think Auntie is our bridge in death as she was once our bridge in life.

And now tonight is the moon viewing. I cannot say that I am looking forward to it, as the Empress Mother shall be directing everything and already the villa is crowded with her noble court ladies, who have not been here all summer. And, of course, all this takes place at the *gepparo* pavilion, which is the one for moon viewing and closest to our apartments. There shall be no escaping.

Later

Normally, *Tsukimi* is one of my favorite celebrations, which marks the end of summer and the beginning of autumn, the most beautiful season in Kyoto. I love the story that is told to children about the rabbit in the moon, and I even love looking for that rabbit with little Sachi. I made him a brush painting of the rabbit this year. We pray for a rich harvest and offer rice dumplings to the moon, and there are vases with lovely grasses arranged in them that catch the silvery light.

It is a celebration I think for everyone — the farmers who harvest the rice, the priests who chant the rice prayers, the small children who believe in the moon rabbit. Usually, we have a farmer as a guest from the Imperial rice paddies, but this year there is not a farmer honored. Why? Because the Empress Mother said so. But the nasty court lady who made the dumpling joke about Lady Tomaki, whom the Emperor banished, is here. I was shocked and so was Mother. When my mother grows extremely nervous, she tucks her lips in and presses them together. She did this so much that the blackening on her teeth wore thin. I noticed it and was about to tell her to retire to touch it up, when something incredibly shocking happened. The Empress Mother noticed, too. She laughed in that way of hers that I hate. It sounds like glass breaking. "Ah!" she said lightly. "She is, in her odd little way, anticipating, I do believe, Chikako's teeth-blackening ceremony come November."

November! That is just two months away. My mother and I were too stunned to say a word. I noticed my brother the Emperor duck his head in a sheepish manner. What a wet rice cake my brother is! Ii Naosuke and the *bakafu* is one thing, but to let his own mother boss him about like that is shameful. What devil's deal has he struck with this woman? Even his wife, Kujo, looked shocked. Without exchanging glances, Mother and I both got up from our places at the pavilion and left. I held my head high. My hair almost brushed the floor. How dare this woman decide when my teeth-blackening ceremony should take place? How dare she take this honor away from my mother? And she will not change my birthday. The first thing I did after going to my apartments was find the poem that Arisugawa sent me for my birthday and reread it.

Later

I have reread that poem so many times. They can try and make me their puppet. They can blacken my teeth. They can change my birthday, but deep inside of me nothing will change. My real birthday will always be my birthday. And although my teeth may appear black, my mother promises me that she will have another ceremony on a date of her choosing. So, you see, no matter how they cut me up to serve their purposes, within me there shall always remain a little spark, a small piece that is my essence and cannot be destroyed no matter what. Perhaps it is the spark of the Fire Horse.

Hazuki August 20, 1858

So astonished was I by the announcement of the teeth-blackening ceremony that I seemed to have forgotten part of its meaning in the Imperial family, which is that a marriage contract would very soon be settled upon. I thought of this some hours later. But neither my mother nor I knew if the contract was to be for a marriage to Yoshi or Arisugawa. Then as we sat there pondering, Keiko came to us. She bowed and gave us a message from Midori, the servant of the Emperor's wife, Kujo. I immediately remembered the look of shock on Empress Kujo's face as her mother-in-law announced the date of my teeth-blackening ceremony. But my own mother was mystified. "The Empress Kujo says that she wants us to meet her at the earthen bridge near Miyuki Lane that leads to a garden seldom used this time of year."

So we went to meet the Empress and in this way I

found out whom I was to marry — Yoshi, now known as the shogun Ieomochi. My mother and I were bewildered. "I thought the shogunate and Ii Naosuke were the Emperor's enemies now that they went against his wishes in signing the treaty," my mother said.

"They were," Empress Kujo answered slowly. "But my husband the Emperor is now completely powerless and there are those who think that it is in everyone's best interests if a bond can be made between the shogunate and the Imperial family."

"My daughter must become the wife of the enemy?" My mother spoke as if she was in a daze.

And even though I felt numb throughout this conversation, my mother's use of the word *enemy* shocked me out of my numbed state. "Honorable Mother," I said. And tears welled in my eyes. "Yoshi is not my enemy. He is my friend, and he shall always be my friend."

"That doesn't matter." My mother's voice was suddenly as heated as I have ever heard it. "You are being used. Used in a terrible way. And what does the Empress Mother think?"

Kujo's face darkened. "The Empress Mother wants power. That is all she cares about. She sees that her son is now completely powerless, but she feels that if some link, some kind of bond can be made between the throne and the shogunate, there is a chance for more power —

especially for herself. She is becoming Ii Naosuke's best friend. And who knows, perhaps more."

"What?" my mother and I both said in a low whisper.

"There are rumors. That is all I can say." Kujo dipped her head but I could see the blood rising in her cheeks despite the thick coating of rice powder.

Then my mother recovered herself. She looked the Empress straight in the eye, which is an unheard-of affront, but the Empress ignored it. "And why do you, Your Highness, come and tell us these things?"

Empress Kujo's eyes filled with tears and she said something extraordinary. "We are but puppets and, like the *bunraku* puppets, even though the operators can be seen, the audience is conditioned to ignore them. I have come to tell you who the operators are: Empress Mother and Ii Naosuke. But more important, I have come to tell you that even though I have been a puppet my entire life I, too, have emotions. When you left this evening, when you showed your true feelings, something leaped up within me. I feel there is some spark of human feeling still in this court. The Empress Mother wants you banished, Kangyoinsan," she spoke, using my mother's name, which is hardly ever spoken by an Empress to one who had been an Emperor's *nyogo*. "And I told His Majesty if they banish you, I shall go into seclusion."

This shocked us entirely. Surely, the Empress Kujo could not mean this. "Going into seclusion" is a kind of court suicide. One does not actually die but one is never seen again. It is a self-imposed banishment that brings nothing but dishonor upon the Imperial family. If, indeed, Kujo were not an Empress and wanted to give up the material world, she could do so with great honor by becoming a Buddhist nun. But she, as a wife of a reigning Emperor, does not have this choice. My mother and I were humbled by this woman and her deep passions. Mother immediately bent to her knees and made the bow of complete obeisance to Empress Kujo. "You honor us with your feelings and your words, Your Majesty," Mother said quietly.

So I conclude, here is another person who has preserved that spark deep within her that is the essence of her being and cannot be destroyed.

Later

I found my mother bent over the orange book of records in which she has so carefully inscribed all of my ceremonies of growing up, from my chopstick ceremony when I was three months old, to my first haircutting the following year, to my good-luck ceremony. She stroked each sheet of paper lovingly.

"Worry not, Mother, I have hope."

And Mother turned to me and said, "No matter what, I shall not record the teeth-blackening ceremony until it is a date of my choosing." And in my mother I began to see a tiny spark glow, and I sensed that it could become a raging fire.

Nagatsuki September 8, 1858
The Time the Wild Geese Fly Over
Imperial Palace, Kyoto

We have been back now for some days. The cool fall winds blow, and I now have Keiko take from my chest the chrysanthemum kimono, for such is the season. I wore the kimono to my meeting with the new shogun, my future husband. We drank tea but it was so unlike tea with Auntie. The Empress Mother sat smiling hard through her black teeth. The Emperor and Ii Naosuke both looked nervous to me. Indeed, the only one who did not look nervous was the Empress Kujo. There is nothing more to report.

Later

There is something more to report! A message came that I was to meet Iemochi — I cannot get used to calling him by that name — in a far garden off the palace grounds. So I did. He immediately dismissed his guard. We were, at first, very shy with each other. Again, what was left unsaid seemed to speak more loudly than what was said. But finally he broke this odd silence with real words.

"Chikako, we are friends are we not?"

"We are to be husband and wife in two years according to the contract."

"Two years is a long time. We must be friends. At least for two years. And I want you to know about Yukiko."

"Who is Yukiko?"

He touched his heart lightly. I inhaled sharply. "The *eta*?" I hardly dared whisper the word.

"She is not unclean, Chikako. She is a good girl whose father happens to be a tanner. The world is changing, Chikako."

"What are you talking about?"

"For hundreds of years Japan has been closed off from the world. Our country might as well have been situated on the moon. I know that the *daimyo* and the samurai have believed in the Emperor forever. 'Long live the Emperor. Throw out the Barbarians.' But the Emperor is the walking dead and you know it. This is his fate. We now have a treaty to trade with England and the Netherlands."

"Netherlands. What are they?"

"A country far away, but nearer than the moon. Chikako, the time has come for us to join the rest of the world — the world that is here on Earth. We Japanese spend countless hours viewing the moon but we must open ourselves to things closer . . . and . . ."

"And what? Have you become a puppet of Ii Naosuke?"

Yoshi's face turned dark with anger. "I hate him."

"You what?"

"You heard me. I dare not repeat it, and there are others who hate him as well. But believe me when I tell you this treaty is not all bad. Not only will it open Japan to the rest of the world, but it will open the court as well, and many of the old ways, the ways that you and I both hate, will begin to fade. We are puppets. You are the one who told me that first, but now there is a chance for the puppets to die."

"But what about . . ." I hesitated. "Yukiko?"

"You are my friend and Yukiko is my love, just as I am your friend and Prince Arisugawa is your love. And are we not richer for being able to even have such people in our lives and the real feelings to cry for both?"

"Yoshi-san," I said. "You are right." And within him I

saw yet another spark that cannot be destroyed. Enough sparks and, yes, a fire might truly ignite.

Kannazuki October 13, 1858

I have not written in this journal for some time. There have been many sadnesses. Lady Tomaki lost her baby. And the Empress Mother can barely conceal her gloating smile. I miss Auntie more than I thought I would. And the cold winds of fall and the mists that so often shroud the gardens seem to increase my longing for her. Spies abound in the court now. Ii Naosuke and the Empress Mother both have many. And although there are rumors that the Empress Mother and Ii Naosuke are extremely close, I do believe that they even set spies upon each other. Spies are everywhere. I have taken to threading a hair through my writing box so that I might tell if it has been disturbed. We prepare now for the Chrysanthemum Festival. This evening outside in the palace gardens, all the chrysanthemum plants are covered in cotton wool to catch the evening and the morning dew. This dew is thought to be magical and can make old people feel and look younger and cure all sorts of ailments. I have some special chrysanthemum plants near my apartments, and I shall gather the cotton wool for my mother and Lady Tomaki.

Kannazuki October 14, 1858

This morning after I delivered the cotton wool to Mother and Lady Tomaki, I took a piece for myself and wiped my face with it. Perhaps it does have magical powers, for a wonderful idea came to me. But I dare not write it down here. For no one, except my mother, must know about it.

And now this evening is the Chrysanthemum Festival. All over the palace grounds, I see the frames for the life-size chrysanthemum dolls being erected and soon the *kiku shi*, the ones who put the flowers into the frames, shall begin to do their work. I do love watching as the chrysanthemum dolls begin to take form.

Later

It is late but I am not that tired from the festival. I think this is because I am so excited about my idea. I told my mother, and it made her very happy. She said that she would get the Empress Kujo's ear and tell her. But I warned her, "Please Mother, make sure no spies are around." She was successful I think, because tonight at the festival, the Empress gave me a quick little wink and a smile. So she must know.

It was a perfect evening for the festival and under the full moon's light the chrysanthemum dolls seemed to come to life. The Empress Mother and the dumpling lady who was banished, Lady Daisho, made several comments about my upcoming teeth-blackening ceremony. "And," the Empress Mother said, stroking her cat Hiroki who curled in her arms, "Lady Daisho has so kindly agreed to be the first blackener. We are already consulting with the astrologers about your new birth date, which shall be announced at the ceremony." I nodded politely and did my best and most perfect bow, very deep to the Empress Mother and a little less deep to Lady Daisho. Then I heard her say as I walked away, "She learns — this one. And she will become even more obedient to me in the future." I cast my eyes down submissively. Inside, the Fire Horse reared.

The ceremony is three weeks away. I shall be very busy between now and then and might not have time to write.

Shimotsuki November 12, 1858

And now, at last, I might write and tell the complete story of my teeth-blackening ceremony. It is one day after what was fixed to be the date by the Empress Mother. But you see, it did not happen then. It had already happened on an equally auspicious day, two days before! Indeed, even more auspicious, for the winds on that day turned in a very lucky direction. Mother and I and the Empress Kujo, who was my first blackener, had secretly consulted with astrologers at the temple of Kennin-ji. Had we consulted with ones here, spies would have heard. Besides, I think that the Empress Mother had bribed them to claim that November 11 was lucky. It was indeed lucky for her and that, of course, was why she wanted the ceremony done on that day. She craved to have the future wife of the shogun in her power. My real teeth-blackening ceremony took place just as I wanted it, with my mother and Lady Tomaki and Empress Kujo. The only person missing was dear Auntie. But Auntie would have approved. A nun from Kennin-ji and a priest were there as well. The ashes had been mixed with the iron dust and rice alcohol and stored in the dark for several days and then brought forth in the same cups that had been used by my mother many years before. I walked into the twelve-mat tatami room. I wore a kimono that was too big for me last year. It is beautiful with plum blossoms and snow and the deep dark green pine boughs — the approved colors of winter. My hair now does not simply touch the tatami mats, but sweeps them. And then, for the first time, like a truly grown-up noble lady, I wore the broad sedge hat with its curtains that drop all the way to the mats. The curtains covered my face entirely until they were lifted by my mother to allow the first blackener, Empress Kujo, to take the brush to my teeth. And thus my teeth-blackening ceremony proceeded. I was given gifts including, among other things, my own small tub and tools for tooth dying, a cosmetic box, and a beautifully illustrated copy of *The Tale of Genji* by Lady Murasaki. Oh, yes, there was even a gift from Auntie that she had selected before she died for when this day would finally come. It is a lovely mirror and mirror stand.

So all that happened on November 9, and then came November 11. I was brought into the Empress Mother's eight-mat tatami room. There, all of her favorite court ladies had gathered, including Lady Daisho, who was to be the first blackener. My heart beat wildly in my chest for soon all would be revealed, and I regretted none of it. How insulting this ceremony was to my mother and myself. My brother the Emperor did not even come because of his anger with his mother. This perhaps has been his most willful act in months. And, as if this were not insulting enough, my mother was not even allowed the honor of lifting the curtains of my sedge hat. But for this I was happy. It was the Empress Mother herself who was to lift my veil.

And so she did! And so I opened my mouth in a half smile. My darkened teeth glistened! *Bushido!* The way of the samurai! Was it not Yoshi who first called me that on the night we had carried away the drunken Hidaki from Lady Tomaki's chambers? *Yes, I am in a battle here, a battle for honor,* I thought. And this is the smile of a warrior. The Empress Mother's eyes turned to stone. She gasped, and then she let out a piercing shriek. At this point, the Empress Kujo stepped forward. "Empress Mother," she spoke so softly no one could hear her but the three of us and Lady Daisho. "To honor one's parents is the highest duty a child can perform. To dishonor one's mother by depriving her of the performance of the teeth-blackening ceremony could cause unspeakable harm to the karma, not of the mother, but of the one who has permitted this dishonor to happen. No one would dream of injuring Empress Mother's karma by allowing this to take place." Empress Kujo backed away and we, my mother and I, followed her out of the room through the sliding paper doors. And that is all we heard — the wisps of the *shoji* screens as we left. For there was only silence — silence as hard as stone.

I see that I have filled this writing case, the one that my mother gave me that was given to her on the occasion of her girl's clothing ceremony. I think that this story is complete now. My new writing case, the one Lady Tomaki gave me, awaits a first sheet of this diary I keep. But I believe I shall stop writing for now and perhaps wait for a new part of my life to begin.

Kisaragi February, 1862

It has been more than three years since I have picked up my brush to write in this diary. Indeed, this is the first sheet of paper to be put in the writing case that Lady Tomaki gave me for my birthday. And my birthday is still my birthday. I keep in my heart my secret love for Arisugawa, but now I've arrived at the eve of my wedding. Four months ago I set off with my attendants and servants to travel the Imperial road, the Nakasendo Road, to the capital city of Edo where my friend, Yoshi, waited for me. Before I left, I met with Arisugawa one last time. We met at the Kamigamo shrine where, at the time of the summer solstice, we had both stepped through the ring of fire and then went to the Nara Brook where we sent the paper figures with our names fluttering down the tumbling waters.

The waters were frozen and there was no ring of fire to step through. The shrine was almost deserted except for the old monks and the nuns. And Arisugawa and I did not bring paper cutout figures to float. Instead, I brought my Auntie's mirror and like the two lovers in the story that was recalled at our first tea ceremony together, we knelt on the banks of the Nara Brook and peered into the mirror where the reflections of both our faces were framed. Then together we buried the mirror and wondered if perhaps a rose might grow there.

I had looked across the brook for the spot where my dear friend Yoshi went with Yukiko. Yes, they came here, too. But you see I no longer call her simply the *eta* girl. And I met her last summer. She has a name. She is an intelligent girl. Indeed, it was Yukiko who reminded me of the story of the *omokage* rose. She had told me it was a favorite of hers. So I thought, as I looked across, that perhaps two roses might grow along the Nara.

"Perhaps." I heard a voice so clear as I walked the twisting path. Why, I do believe it was the spirit of Auntie.

EPILOGUE

"Without thought of myself, for you my lord and your people, I will evaporate with the dew . . ." So wrote Kazunomiya in a poem about her decision to submit to her brother's wishes and marry the shogun Iemochi and leave Kyoto, the city she loved, for Edo, the city that she intensely disliked, now called Tokyo.

In 1861, Kazunomiya journeyed from Kyoto to Edo along the famous Imperial road known as the Nakasendo. It was a very public journey for it was designed to set the people's mind at ease and stabilize the political situation by showing the future union of the Imperial court and the shogunate through the marriage of Kazunomiya and Iemochi. It was an immense bridal procession that required twelve thousand people to travel first from Edo to Kyoto to fetch the Princess, and an additional ten thousand to accompany her back to the capital. Indeed, the procession was so huge that it strained the towns and villages along the route. It was recorded that these towns and villages had to supply more than one thousand porters and hundreds of horses when the procession arrived. Thus, men and animals were drafted into service from other villages. It is not surprising that the strain was resented by the people and undercut the political intentions of the marriage, which was supposed to set their minds at ease. Nonetheless, there were monuments built to commemorate the Princess's journey. At the top of one mountain pass, the Biwa, it is told that she turned and looked back at her beloved Kyoto to recite a poem of farewell that she had composed. The poem was inscribed on a rock at this pass and can be seen to this day. All along the Nakasendo, Kazunomiya wrote poems that mostly focused on leaving and longing for her old city, such as those which follow:

> *Leaving the city of my birth*
> *after many days*
> *I hurriedly approach*
> *this journey to the east*

> *I know what it is like*
> *for the flow of pure water*
> *that will never again*
> *return to its source*

The falling leaves
of autumn
make the body
yearn for the past

The marriage between Kazunomiya and the young shogun Tokugawa Iemochi took place in March of 1862. Iemochi lived for only another four years, dying in 1866. It is not known if Kazunomiya's marriage was a happy one or not, or if she ever again saw Prince Arisugawa. It was rumored that she did not get along with her mother-in-law. It has been noted by historians that since she was the first daughter of an Emperor to ever have married a shogun, she was very intent on maintaining her Imperial status by insisting on following "court style" and using her Imperial title. This suggests that Kazunomiya did feel superior to her mother-in-law and her husband, who could not, as royalty could, claim descent from the divine sun goddess, Amaterasu.

After his death, Ieomochi was succeeded as shogun by Tokugawa Yoshinobu. But this, the fifteenth shogun's rule, would not be long. In 1868, the shogunate came to an end for good when a coup d'etat was initiated and a new form of governmnet was installed. This period is referred to as the Restoration, for, in fact, the Emperor was restored to the throne with full powers. And the Emperor was none other than Kazunomiya's little nephew Sachi, who was then fifteen years old. Kazunomiya was very important to the success of the new Imperial government. A proclamation issued on January 3, 1868, stated that, with the surrender of the shogun, the Princess Kazunomiya must go to Kyoto as quickly as possible.

It would be a year, however, before Kazunomiya finally returned for good to her beloved Kyoto, where she entered a Buddhist monastery of the Seigô'in temple. She immediately pursued her poetry and calligraphy. Most of Kazunomiya's poetry dates from the last few years of her life. She died in 1877 and was buried, it was thought, with her husband at the Zojoji temple in Shiba. There was, however, an intriguing mystery that was literally uncovered years later when graves in this burial ground were removed to make way for the Prince Hotel in the early 1950s. The body of Kazunomiya was among those disinterred. When archeologists examined the remains in the coffin, it was found the dead woman was missing her left hand. Could the hand have simply disintegrated after the eighty years of internment when the coffin itself was exposed to the elements? Or was it the real Kazunomiya? Some have speculated that the Princess exchanged places with another woman, an imposter, as she traveled along the Nakasendo Road. But there is some evidence that Kazunomiya might, in fact, have been missing a hand. In a bronze statue commissioned a few years after her death, she is shown with her left hand deep within the folds of her robes.

There was still another puzzling mystery that was revealed from the excavation of the graves. The custom was for a widow to cut her hair at the time of her husband's death and for that hair to be buried with the husband. It was discovered that the hair in the coffin of Ieomochi was not that of Kazunomiya.

Today, about two thousand of of the *waka* poems that Princess Kazunomiya wrote still exist.

Life in Japan
in 1858

HISTORICAL NOTE

By the time Princess Kazunomiya was born in 1846, Japan had been isolated under its policy of the Chained-in Country, or *sakoku*, for more than two hundred years. The early Japanese rulers had watched with great concern as European missionaries and traders made their way through the countries of Southeast Asia, trying to establish the foundations for European rule. After a combined Christian and peasant rebellion broke out on the southern Japanese island of Kyushu in 1638, Christianity was banned altogether, and the country was closed to foreigners the following year. Then, with the exception of a Dutch trading post on the small man-made island of Deshima, no one could enter or leave Japan but on pain of death. At the farthest western reaches of Asia, and separated from its closest civilized neighbor by the Straits of Tsushima, Japan had always been considered a far-off country by Europeans and Asians alike. Now its isolation seemed to be complete, and news of the outside world was nearly silenced.

The court in which Kazunomiya lived until she was sixteen was a combination of an unbroken line of Emperors that dated from about the third century AD and powerful aristocratic families who had intermarried with the royal line. From about the eighth or ninth century AD, the Emperor and his immediate family had become little more than figureheads, as first the powerful aristocrats, then the warrior clans — or shogunates — took the reins of the government.

Most of the court ceremonies were conducted by the Emperor and his chief ministers, which is to say, by men. Although the women of the court were allowed to attend certain festivals and outings to Buddhist temples, they spent much of their time confined to the palaces. A number of them spent their leisure at writing and other artistic endeavors, however, and produced some of Japan's greatest literary classics, including Lady Murasaki's *The Tale of Genji*, the world's first novel. Virtually all ladies and gentlemen of the court practiced the art of poetry, particularly the *waka*, and this tradition continued throughout the centuries. Princess Kazunomiya herself was well-known for the beauty and sensitivity of the *waka* she wrote.

So in this way, Princess Kazunomiya was born into an isolated world, separated from international, national, and sometimes even court affairs. Nevertheless, it would be a mistake to think that women's life in the court was totally cut off: Many of the court ladies were intelligent, curious, and resourceful, and found their own ways to become informed of what was happening beyond their constrained lives within the palaces.

Conditions that would lead to the breakdown of Japan's isolation started to appear when foreigners began to visit Japanese shores. By the early 1800s, American, British, French, and Russian ships were all demanding the right to stop in Japanese ports for fuel and supplies. When they were refused, the sailors sometimes just took what they wanted, anyway. To add to this, there were occasions when shipwrecked sailors needed aid from the Japanese, but because of the Chained-in Country policy they were either turned away or mistreated. As ship traffic around Japan increased, unpleasant incidents occurred more and more often.

This increased contact with the world outside Japan had far-reaching effects on the country and its people. Although the vast majority of Japanese people never had an opportunity to see these foreigners, the thought of strange people trying to enter their land was unsettling. During this time, some wood-block prints began to depict monsters like giant spiders or ghosts, and by the middle of the century, folktales about the appearance and crimes of foreigners began to spread throughout the country.

On the other hand, advances were being made in scientific areas, as books from the Dutch colony on Deshima were translated into Japanese and applied to the fields of medicine and agriculture. In the art world, wood-block printers were experimenting with the new ideas of perspective they were learning from European painting. Even the shogunate realized that there was much to learn from these foreign people, and as early as 1811, established the Bureau for Translation of Barbarian Writings, which would later become the University of Tokyo.

Finally, on July 8, 1853, the American Admiral Matthew C. Perry arrived with two frigates and two sailboats and demanded a treaty with the Japanese government. The black color and the great size of Perry's boats were very intimidating, but the shogunate refused to cooperate. Perry left, but returned the following February with nine of the great black ships. Displaying this overwhelming power, within a month Perry forced the shogunate to sign a treaty allowing Americans to refuel and trade at the port cities of Shimoda and Hakodate.

Two years later, another American envoy, Townsend Harris, arrived and secured a formal treaty opening up Japan even more. In Japan, this treaty was considered a terrible humiliation and provoked protests across the country. Emperor Komei at first refused to sign it and criticized the shogun for doing so. Respect for the Emperor and disgust with the shogunate had grown apace, and the situation was now critical. In desperation, the shogunate decided that blurring the distinction between court and shogun might ease tension in the country. So Princess Kazunomiya was chosen to be married to the young new shogun, Iemochi, even though she was already engaged to court noble Prince Arisugawa. In the winter of 1861, Kazunomiya began the three-hundred-mile trip from Kyoto to Edo on the Nakasendo Road, a sometimes steep and narrow passage that led through the central mountains of Japan. Her huge entourage greatly overburdened the travel stations and villages along the way, as they were forced to provide thousands of horses and porters, and extra provisions. This further provoked the people against the shogun's government. Eighty days later, Kazunomiya arrived at Edo castle and became the wife of the shogun.

This ploy did not work. The Emperor objected to sending his sister away from Kyoto, and the court grew increasingly hostile and radical. The slogan that had been so popular "Respect the Emperor. Throw out the foreigners" now quickly changed to "Respect the Emperor. Overthrow the shogunate." Samurai from the southwestern parts of Japan that had begun to buy Western ships and weapons, now began to visit the court and express their solidarity with the Emperor. It was time to make a new Japan by going back to the ancient government of the Imperial court. The confusion and violence that ensued did not last long. In 1868, both the Emperor and the shogun died of smallpox; within a year, the final shogun was forced to resign. The new Emperor, Mutsubito, or the Emperor Meiji as he would be called, took the reins of the government and the Restoration began.

As the Imperial Restoration progressed, it very quickly became clear that it would not take the direction that so many had wanted. Instead of throwing out the foreigners, the new leaders of the country realized that if Japan was to survive in the modern world, it would need all of the foreign technology it could learn. This required both the importation of foreign teachers and the search for knowledge abroad. This search, moreover, extended not just to the military but to politics, education, and economics as well. The warriors who had fought so bravely for the Emperor lost their right to carry swords, and an army that required all men to serve three years as soldiers was created. At last, the class system was abolished altogether, and the court itself, with the exception of the Emperor and his immediate family, was gone.

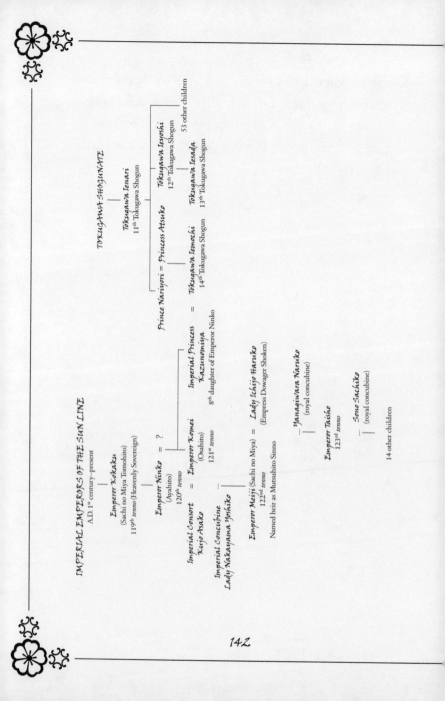

IMPERIAL EMPERORS OF THE SUN LINE
A.D. 1st century–present

TOKUGAWA SHOGUNATE

KAZUNOMIYA'S FAMILY TREE

THE IMPERIAL DYNASTY,

THE EMPERORS OF THE SUN LINE

The Sun Line (or Yamato Line) is the oldest continuous line of Japanese monarchs. The Sun Emperors are said to be descendants of Amaterasu-Omikami, the sun goddess, and Kyoto was their Imperial city.

Emperor Kokaku

The one hundred nineteenth tenno was born in 1771 and named Sachi-no-Miya Tomohito. He married the daughter of the one hundred eighteenth tenno, Emperor Go-Momozono (r. 1771–79). Kokaku was emperor for thirty-seven years. His son became Emperor Ninko, who reigned for twenty-nine years.

Emperor Komei

The son and heir to Emperor Ninko and grandson of Emperor Kokaku, Komei was born in 1831 and given the name Osahito. Komei was a figurehead with no real power at a time of great change and unrest in Japan. He died on January 30, 1867, in Kyoto.

Kazunomiya, Imperial Princess

Princess Kazunomiya was born in 1846, the year her father, Emperor Ninko, died and her half brother Komei became Emperor. On October 20, 1861, at age fifteen, she began the difficult journey from Kyoto east to Edo for her wedding to Shogun Iemochi.

When Iemochi died suddenly in 1866, Princess Kazunomiya remained in Edo and became a Buddhist nun. The following year the shogunate was defeated in battle. Kazunomiya pleaded for merciful treatment for the Tokugawa family. It is believed that she died in or around 1877 and is remembered for the strength of her character.

Sachi-no-Miya, Emperor Meiji

Born on November 3, 1852, Prince Sachi was made the official heir to the throne at age eight, and he ascended the throne on February 3, 1867. He was named Meiji, or "enlightened ruler." By November of the same year, the final Tokugawa shogun surrendered the shogunate to the Emperor, and the "old monarchy" was restored by the *Sonno Joi* ("Revere the Emperor. Expel the Barbarians.") movement.

Under Emperor Meiji, Japan became a constitutional state, trade was opened, and industry and the military were modernized. He and his wife, the Lady Ichijo Haruko, became symbols of the nation. They had no children, but Emperor Meiji had concubines with whom he had fifteen children. His son and heir, Yoshihito, the Emperor Taisho, was born to Imperial Concubine Yanagiwara Naruko. Meiji died after a long illness in 1912, which brought the Meiji Era to a close.

THE TOKUGAWA DYNASTY

The Tokugawa shogunate was the last of three warrior governments, called *bakufu* ("tent governments"), to govern Japan.

Ienari, Eleventh Tokugawa shogun

Ienari (1773–1841) was named heir to the childless tenth shogun, Ieharu. He became shogun at age thirteen and held his title longer — fifty years — than any other shogun in the Tokugawa line, from 1787 to 1837.

He used marriages, adoptions, and family obligations to spread his power. It is reported that Ienari had fifty-five children, whom he placed at the head of the three main branches of the Tokugawa family as well as in its many noble houses and minor branches.

Prince Nariyori

Prince Tokugawa Nariyori (1801–1846) was the brother of Shogun Ieyoshi, who was the second son of Shogun Ienari. Prince Nariyori, one of Ienari's younger sons, was *daimyo* or Lord of the Kii, one of the main branches of the Tokugawa family. Nariyori was married to Princess Atsuko.

Iemochi, Fourteenth Tokugawa shogun

Tokugawa Yoshitomi was born in 1846 to the Kii noble house. He was named shogun in 1858, but he was not an able leader.

Princess Kazunomiya married Iemochi on March 11, 1862, in Edo. They were both sixteen years old. This political marriage did not solve the weakness of the shogunate, however.

Iemochi died unexpectedly of unknown causes on August 29, 1866, while staying overnight at Osaka Castle on his way to Choshu district to fight the forces battling the shogunate.

One of a few existing photographs of Princess Kazunomiya.

Prince Arisugawa was a Japanese court noble who was engaged to Kazunomiya, until she was chosen to marry the young shogun Iemochi.

Tokugawa Yoshitomi, who was called Iemochi, was named shogun in 1858, and was married to Kazunomiya at the age of sixteen.

A parchment bearing Kazunomiya's calligraphy.

A photograph of Princess Kazunomiya's travel toiletries kit.

A modern-day photograph of the Japanese Imperial palace at Katsura. The palace was designed to be used between spring and autumn. The lush gardens were complete with strolling paths, riding grounds, and a large pond for boating, as well as a dramatic setting for tea ceremonies.

This woodcut shows three women engaging in a traditional tea ceremony. The ceremony takes place in a room designed and designated specifically to allow participants to achieve inner peace through the simple act of preparing the tea.

Early sumo wrestling matches were dedicated to the gods in prayer for a good harvest, and the oldest written records of sumo matches date all the way back to the eighth century A.D. Sumo wrestling matches are accompanied by a great deal of traditional ceremony, but the match itself is comprised of pushing or throwing one's opponent out of the doyo, *or ring, or trying to pull him down to the floor.*

GLOSSARY OF
JAPANESE WORDS

Amaterasu: divine sun goddess in Shinto religion
bakufu: the shogun's government
beya: school or training ground for the wrestlers
bunraku: theater using large puppets where the operators can be seen
bushido: The way of the samurai
chado: the way of tea, same as chanoyu
chanko nabe: the hearty stew that all sumo wrestlers eat
chanoyu: way of tea ceremony
daimyo: lord
dharma: Buddha's teachings
eta: an outcast, lower class of people
genza: an exorcist
Gion: part of Kyoto where geishas live, known as the Floating World
gosho: palace
hanto: assistant to the tea master
Heian times: (AD 794–1192) period in Japanese history under the powerful rule of the Heian dynasty
hosodono: the main meditation hall
Inari: fox shrine

kagami: mirror
kaiseki: traditional temple food
kami: god
kayari: incense to kill mosquitoes; incense coil
kimono: Japanese robe
koto: stringed musical instrument
Kyoto Gosho: Heavenly Palace, home of the Emperor in Kyoto
michiyuki: outing
miso: soybean paste soup
mochi: rice cake
Nagashi bina: a ceremony, floating dolls down the stream to send them to heaven
Nakasendo: road through the mountains from Kyoto to the capitol city of Edo
ningyo: doll
nishibashi: where many of the court ladies and the nyogo live
nyogo: favorite consort of royalty, not a wife
ofuro: hot bath
omokage: rose name which means memory of face
Otsune-goten: everyday palace

puja: an offering to Buddha

rikishi: wrestlers

roji: tea ceremony garden path

sakoku: closed country, forbidden land, Chained-in Country

samurai: Japanese warriors or knights

sangha: part of Buddhism, one's commitment to the community and not just individuals

sensei: teacher or master

Sento gosho: the palace for the retired Emperor

Shinto: traditional religion

shogun: barbarian-expelling warlord, most powerful man in feudal Japan

shogunate: rule by the shogun

shobu-sake: a potent drink, leaves of iris soaked in rice wine

Sonnoi Joi: movement to revere the Emperor

sumi-e: ink paintings

Tanabata: star festival

Tango No Sekku: Boys' Day Celebration

tatami: straw mat used as flooring in a Japanese home

tokonoma: alcove in a Japanese room usually used to show a few beautiful objects

torii: symbolic gate marking a sacred place in Shinto

tsubone: the lower ranked court ladies

Tsukimi: moon-viewing celebration that marks the end of summer and the beginning of autumn, the most beautiful season of Kyoto

ubone: cormorant fishing boat

ukai: fishing expedition using cormorants

usho: bird handler

wabi: beauty and order that exist beneath the surface of things, the heart of tea ceremony

waka: thirty-one-syllable poems

yama: mountain

yukata: cotton robe to wear while bathing

ABOUT THE AUTHOR

Kathryn Lasky traveled to Japan during the time she was writing Kazunomiya's story. She spent most of her time in Kyoto visiting the temples, the gardens, and some of the palaces in which Kazunomiya lived or spent time. Because fire was so prevalent in those days, many of the palaces had burned and had been rebuilt since the time of Kazunomiya.

This was Ms. Lasky's first trip to Japan, although she has long been fascinated by Japanese culture. Perhaps she was most intrigued by what she calls "the deep aesthetic" that is such an integral part of Japanese life, which is evident "in everything from the way they arrange rocks in a garden, to food on a plate, and the pouring of tea into a bowl." Her husband, Christopher Knight, had been to Japan as a photographer for *National Geographic* magazine many years before. He had learned and not forgotten some Japanese, which was quite helpful. But both Ms. Lasky and her husband wish to thank William Wilson, their old friend, who accompanied them for much of their trip. Mr. Wilson is a Japanese scholar and translator of classical Japanese literature. He speaks fluent Japanese and has also written the historical note for this diary. Ms. Lasky is also indebted to Mark Brewer, who is one of the foremost scholars of Kazunomiya's poetry and who was well-acquainted with many of the more obscure details of Kazunomiya's life. In addition to William Wilson and Mark Brewer, Kathryn Lasky is especially grateful to her friend Keiko Thayer, who helped her understand court life, offered instant translations when necessary, and provided her with an invaluable catalog from a museum exhibition some years ago in Tokyo of Kazunomiya's personal articles. Ms. Lasky says, "Good books are often a collaboration and this diary certainly was one. I could not have done it without these people."

Kathryn Lasky is the author of more than forty books for children and adults, including *Sofia's Immigrant Diaries* for the My America series; *Elizabeth I, Jahanara, Marie Antoinette,* and *Mary, Queen of Scots* for The Royal Diaries series; several books for the Dear America series, including *A Journey to the New World, Dreams in the Golden Country, Christmas After All,* and *A Time for Courage*; and *The Journal of Augustus Pelletier* for the My Name Is America series. She is also the author of *Beyond the Burning Time, True North,* and the Newbery Honor book *Sugaring Time.*

ACKNOWLEDGMENTS

Grateful acknowledgment is made for permission to reprint the following:

Cover painting by Tim O'Brien

Page 147, Princess Kazunomiya, The Tokugawa Memorial Foundation, Japan.

Page 148, top: Prince Arisugawa, Old Japan Picture Library, Surrey, England.

Page 148, bottom: Tokugawa Yoshitomi (Iemochi), The Tokugawa Memorial Foundation, Japan.

Page 149, top: Kazunomiya's calligraphy, The Tokugawa Memorial Foundation, Japan.

Page 149, bottom: Kazunomiya's toiletries, The Tokugawa Memorial Foundation, Japan.

Page 150, top: The Imperial palace at Katsura, Horace Bristol/Corbis, New York.

Page 150, bottom: Traditonal tea ceremony, Colored woodcut by Inoue Shinshichi, Photo by Juergen Liepe. Copyright Bildarchiv Pressischer Kulturbesitz/Art Resource, New York.

Page 151: Sumo wrestlers, Old Japan, Surrey, England.

OTHER BOOKS IN THE ROYAL DIARIES SERIES

Copyright © 2004 by Kathryn Lasky

All rights reserved. Published by Scholastic Inc.
557 Broadway, New York, New York 10012.
SCHOLASTIC, THE ROYAL DIARIES, and associated logos are trademarks and/or registered trademarks of Scholastic Inc.

Library of Congress Cataloging-in-Publication Data
Lasky, Kathryn.
Kazunomiya : prisoner of heaven / by Kathryn Lasky.
p. cm. — (The Royal Diaries)
Summary: Princess Kazunomiya, half-sister of the Emperor of Japan, relates in her diary and in poems the confusing events occurring in the Imperial palace in 1858, including political and romantic intrigue.
ISBN 0-439-16485-0
[1. Seikan'in no Miya, 1846–1877 — Juvenile fiction. 2. Kazunomiya, Princess of Japan, 1846–1877 — Juvenile fiction. 3. Princesses — Fiction.
4. Diaries — Fiction. 5. Japan — History — Tokugawa period, 1600–1868 — Juvenile fiction. 6. Japan — History — Tokugawa period, 1600–1868 — Fiction.]
I. Title. II. Series.
PZ7.L3274 Kaz 2004
[Fic] 22   2003025474
10 9 8 7 6 5 4 3 2 1   04 05 06 07 08

The display type was set in Vinerhand
The text type was set in Augereau
Book design by Steve Hughes
Photo research by Amla Sanghvi

Printed in the U.S.A.
First edition, September 2004